New York Times bestselling author and MWA Grandmaster Ed McBain has gathered ten masters of modern fiction and had them each write a novella for this one-of-a-kind series. Look for more *Transgressions* featuring new tales from these bestselling authors:

Lawrence Block

Jeffery Deaver

John Farris

Stephen King

Ed McBain

Sharyn McCrumb

Walter Mosley

Joyce Carol Oates

Anne Perry

Donald E. Westlake

TRANSGRESSIONS

Edited by Ed McBain

THE THINGS THEY
LEFT BEHIND
Stephen King

THE RANSOME WOMEN
John Farris

FORGE®

A TOM DOHERTY ASSOCIATES BOOK
NEW YORK

Copyright Acknowledgments

"The Things They Left Behind," copyright © 2005 by Stephen King
"The Ransome Women," copyright © 2005 by John Farris

This is a work of fiction. All the characters and events portrayed in this book are either products of the author's imagination or are used fictitiously.

TRANSGRESSIONS

The novellas collected in this volume and the three companion volumes of *Transgressions* were previously published in 2005 as a single-volume hardcover edition under the title *Transgressions*.

A Forge Book
Published by Tom Doherty Associates, LLC
175 Fifth Avenue
New York, NY 10010

www.tor.com

Forge® is a registered trademark of Tom Doherty Associates, LLC.

ISBN-13: 978-0-765-34751-0
ISBN-10: 0-765-34751-2

First mass market edition: September 2006

Printed in the United States of America

0 9 8 7 6 5 4 3 2 1

Contents

Introduction

When I was writing novellas for the pulp magazines back in the 1950s, we still called them "novelettes," and all I knew about the form was that it was long and it paid half a cent a word. This meant that if I wrote 10,000 words, the average length of a novelette back then, I would sooner or later get a check for five hundred dollars. This was not bad pay for a struggling young writer.

A novella today can run anywhere from 10,000 to 40,000 words. Longer than a short story (5,000 words) but much shorter than a novel (at least 60,000 words), it combines the immediacy of the former with the depth of the latter, and it ain't easy to write. In fact, given the difficulty of the form, and the scarcity of markets for novellas, it is surprising that any writers today are writing them at all.

But here was the brilliant idea.

Round up the best writers of mystery, crime, and suspense novels, and ask them to write a brand-new novella for a collection of similarly superb novellas to be published anywhere in the world for the very first time. Does that sound keen, or what? In a perfect world, *yes*, it *is* a wonderful idea, and here is your novella, sir, thank you very much for asking me to contribute.

But many of the bestselling novelists I approached had never written a novella in their lives. (Some of them had never even written a short story!) Up went the hands in mock horror. "What! A novella? I wouldn't even know how to *begin* one." Others thought that writing a novella ("*How* long did you say it had to be?") would constitute a wonderful challenge, but bestselling novelists are busy people with publishing contracts to fulfill and deadlines to meet, and however intriguing the invitation may have seemed at first, stark reality reared its ugly head, and so . . .

"Gee, thanks for thinking of me, but I'm already three months behind deadline," or . . .

"My publisher would *kill* me if I even dreamed of writing something for another house," or . . .

"Try me again a year from now," or . . .

"Have you asked X? Or Y? Or Z?"

What it got down to in the end was a matter of timing and luck. In some cases, a writer I desperately wanted was happily between novels and just happened to have some free time on his/her hands. In other cases, a writer had an idea that was too short for a novel but too long for a short story, so yes, what a wonderful opportunity! In yet other cases, a writer wanted to introduce a new character he or she had been thinking about for some time. In each and every case, the formidable task of writing fiction that fell somewhere between 10,000 and 40,000 words seemed an exciting challenge, and the response was enthusiastic.

Except for length and a loose adherence to crime, mystery, or suspense, I placed no restrictions upon the writers who agreed to contribute. The results are as astonishing as they are brilliant. The novellas that follow are as varied as the writers who concocted them, but they all exhibit the same devoted passion and the same extraordinary writing. More than that, there is an underlying sense here that the writer is attempting something new and unexpected, and willing to share his or her own surprises with us. Just as their names are in alphabetical order on the book cover, so do their stories follow in reverse alphabetical order: I have no favorites among them. I love them all equally.

Enjoy!

ED MCBAIN
Weston, Connecticut
August 2004

TRANSGRESSIONS

STEPHEN KING

There are certain things that are almost always mentioned when the name **Stephen King** comes up. How many books he's sold. What he's doing in and for literature today. One thing almost never mentioned—and not generally perceived—is that he single-handedly made popular fiction grow up. While there were many good bestselling writers before him, King, more than anybody since John D. MacDonald, brought reality to genre novels with his minutely detailed examinations of life and the people of mythical towns in New England that seem to exist due to his amazing talent for making them real in every detail. Of course, combined with the elements of supernatural terror, novels such as *It, The Stand, Insomnia*, and *Bag of Bones* have propelled him to the top of the bestseller lists time after time. He's often remarked that *Salem's Lot* was "Peyton Place Meets Dracula." And so it was. The rich characterization, the careful and caring social eye, the interplay of story line and character development announced that writers could take worn themes such as vampirism or ghosts and make them fresh again. Before King, many popular writers found their efforts to make their books serious blue-penciled by their editors. Stuff like that gets in the way of the story, they were told. Well, it's stuff like that that has made King so popular, and helped free the popular name from the shackles of simple genre writing. He is a master of masters. His most recent novel is *Cell*.

THE THINGS THEY
LEFT BEHIND

Stephen King

The things I want to tell you about—the ones they left behind—showed up in my apartment in August of 2002. I'm sure of that, because I found most of them not long after I helped Paula Robeson with her air conditioner. Memory always needs a marker, and that's mine. She was a children's book illustrator, good-looking (hell, *fine*-looking), husband in import-export. A man has a way of remembering occasions when he's actually able to help a good-looking lady in distress (even one who keeps assuring you she's "very married"); such occasions are all too few. These days the would-be knight errant usually just makes matters worse.

She was in the lobby, looking frustrated, when I came down for an afternoon walk. I said *Hi, howya doin'*, the way you do to other folks who share your building, and she asked me in an exasperated tone that stopped just short of querulousness why the super had to be on vacation *now*. I pointed out that even cowgirls get the blues and even supers go on vacation; that August, furthermore, was an extremely logical month to take time off. August in New York (and in Paris, *mon ami*) finds psychoanalysts, trendy artists, and building superintendents mighty thin on the ground.

She didn't smile. I'm not sure she even got the Tom Robbins reference (obliqueness is the curse of the reading class). She said it might be true about August being a good month to take off and go to the Cape or Fire Island, but her damned apartment was just about burning *up* and the damned air conditioner wouldn't so much as burp. I asked her if she'd like me to take a look, and I remember the glance she gave me—those cool, assessing gray eyes. I remember thinking that eyes like that probably saw quite a lot. And I remember smiling at what she asked me: *Are you safe?* It reminded me of that movie, not *Lolita* (thinking about *Lolita*, sometimes at two in the morning, came later) but the one where Laurence Olivier does the impromptu dental work on Dustin Hoffman, asking him over and over again, *Is it safe?*

I'm safe, I said. *Haven't attacked a woman in over a year. I used to attack two or three a week, but the meetings are helping.*

A giddy thing to say, but I was in a fairly giddy mood. A *summer* mood. She gave me another look, and then *she* smiled. Put out her hand. *Paula Robeson,* she said. It was the left hand she put out—not normal, but the one with the plain gold band on it. I think that was probably on purpose, don't you? But it was later that she told me about her husband being in import-export. On the day when it was my turn to ask *her* for help.

In the elevator, I told her not to expect too much. Now, if she'd wanted a man to find out the underlying causes of the New York City Draft Riots, or to supply a few amusing anecdotes about the creation of the small-pox vaccine, or even to dig up quotes on the sociological ramifications of the TV remote control (the most important invention of the last fifty years, in my 'umble opinion), I was the guy.

Research is your game, Mr. Staley? she asked as we went up in the slow and clattery elevator.

I admitted that it was, although I didn't add that I was still quite new to it. Nor did I ask her to call me Scott—that would have spooked her all over again. And I certainly didn't tell her that I was trying to forget all I'd once known about rural insurance. That I was, in fact, trying to forget quite a lot of things, including about two dozen faces.

You see, I may be trying to forget, but I still remember quite a lot. I think we all do when we put our minds to it (and sometimes, rather more nastily, when we don't). I even remember something one of those South American novelists said—you know, the ones they call the Magical Realists? Not the guy's name, that's not important, but this quote: *As infants, our first victory comes in grasping some bit of the world, usually our mothers' fingers. Later we discover that the world, and the things of the world, are grasping us, and have been all along.* Borges? Yes, it might have been Borges. Or it might have been Marquez. That I *don't* remember. I just know I got her air conditioner running, and when cool air started blowing out of the convector, it lit up her whole face. I also know it's true, that thing about how perception switches around and we come to realize that the things we thought we were holding are actually holding us. Keeping us prisoner, perhaps—Thoreau certainly thought so—but also holding us in place. That's the trade-off. And no matter what Thoreau might have thought, I believe the trade is mostly a fair one. Or I did then; now, I'm not so sure.

And I know these things happened in late August of 2002, not quite a year after a piece of the sky fell down and everything changed for all of us.

On an afternoon about a week after Sir Scott Staley donned his Good Samaritan armor and successfully battled the fearsome air conditioner, I took my afternoon walk to the Staples on 83rd Street to get a box of Zip disks and a ream of paper. I owed a fellow forty pages of background on the development of the Polaroid camera (which is more interesting a story than you might think). When I got back to my apartment, there was a pair of sunglasses with red frames and very distinctive lenses on the little table in the foyer where I keep bills that need to be paid, claim checks, overdue-book notices, and things of that nature. I recognized the glasses at once, and all the strength went out of me. I didn't fall, but I dropped my packages on the floor and leaned against the side of the door, trying to catch my breath and staring at those sunglasses. If there had been nothing to lean against, I believe I would have swooned like a miss in a Victorian novel—one of those where the lustful vampire appears at the stroke of midnight.

Two related but distinct emotional waves struck me. The first was that sense of horrified shame you feel when you know you're about to be caught in some act you will never be able to explain. The memory that comes to mind in this regard is of a thing that happened to me—or almost happened—when I was sixteen.

My mother and sister had gone shopping in Portland and I supposedly had the house to myself until evening. I was reclining naked on my bed with a pair of my sister's underpants wrapped around my cock. The bed was scattered with pictures I'd clipped from magazines I'd found in the back of the garage—the previous owner's stash of *Penthouse* and *Gallery* magazines, very likely. I heard a car come crunching into the driveway. No mistaking the sound of that motor; it was my mother and sister. Peg had come down with some sort of flu bug and started vomiting out the window. They'd gotten as far as Poland Springs and turned around.

I looked at the pictures scattered all over the bed, my clothes scattered all over the floor, and the foam of pink rayon in my left hand. I remember how the strength flowed out of my body, and the terrible sense of lassitude that came in its place. My mother was yelling for me—"Scott, Scott, come down and help me with your sister, she's sick"—and I remember thinking, "What's the use? I'm caught. I might as well accept it, I'm caught and this is the first thing they'll think of when they think about me for the rest of my life: Scott, the jerk-off artist."

But more often than not a kind of survival overdrive kicks in at such moments. That's what happened to me. I might go down, I decided, but I wouldn't do so without at least an effort to save my dignity. I threw the pictures and the panties under the bed. Then I jumped into my clothes, moving with numb but sure-fingered speed, all the time thinking of this crazy old game show I used to watch, *Beat the Clock.*

I can remember how my mother touched my flushed cheek when I got downstairs, and the thoughtful concern in her eyes. "Maybe you're getting sick, too," she said.

"Maybe I am," I said, and gladly enough. It was half an hour before I discovered I'd forgotten to zip my fly. Luckily, neither Peg nor my mother noticed, although on any other occasion one or both of them would have asked me if I had a license to sell hot dogs (this was what passed for wit in the house where I grew up). That day one of them was too sick and the other was too worried to be witty. So I got a total pass.

Lucky me.

What followed the first emotional wave that August day in my apartment was much simpler: I thought I was going out of my mind. Because those glasses couldn't be there. Absolutely could not. No way.

Then I raised my eyes and saw something else that had most certainly not been in my apartment when I left for Staples half an hour before (locking the door behind me, as I always did). Leaning in the corner between the kitchenette and the living room was a baseball bat. Hillerich & Bradsby, according to the label. And while I couldn't see the other side, I knew what was printed there well enough: CLAIMS ADJUSTOR, the words burned into the ash with the tip of a soldering iron and then colored deep blue.

Another sensation rushed through me: a third wave. This was a species of surreal dismay. I don't believe in ghosts, but I'm sure that at that moment I looked as though I had just seen one.

I felt that way, too. Yes indeed. Because those sunglasses had to be gone—long-time gone, as the Dixie Chicks say. Ditto Cleve Farrell's Claims Adjustor. ("Besboll been bery-bery good to mee," Cleve would sometimes say, waving the bat over his head as he sat at his desk. "In-SHOO-rance been bery-bery bad.")

I did the only thing I could think of, which was to grab up Sonja D'Amico's shades and trot back down to the elevator with them, holding them out in front of me the way you might hold out something nasty you found on your apartment floor after a week away on vacation—a piece of decaying food, or the body of a poisoned mouse. I found myself remembering a conversation I'd had about Sonja with a fellow named Warren Anderson. *She must have looked like she thought she was going to pop back up and ask somebody for a Coca-Cola,* I had thought when he told me what he'd seen. Over drinks in the Blarney Stone Pub on Third Avenue, this had been, about six weeks after the sky fell down. After we'd toasted each other on not being dead.

Things like that have a way of sticking, whether you want them to or not. Like a musical phrase or the nonsense chorus to a pop song that you just can't get out of your head. You wake up at three in the morning, needing to take a leak, and as you stand there in front of the bowl, your cock in your hand and your mind about ten percent awake, it comes back to you: *Like she thought she was going to pop back up. Pop back up and ask for a Coke.* At some point during that conversation

Warren had asked me if I remembered her funny sunglasses, and I said I did. Sure I did.

Four floors down, Pedro the doorman was standing in the shade of the awning and talking with Rafe the FedEx man. Pedro was a serious hardboy when it came to letting deliverymen stand in front of the building— he had a seven-minute rule, a pocket watch with which to enforce it, and all the beat cops were his buddies—but he got on with Rafe, and sometimes the two of them would stand there for twenty minutes or more with their heads together, doing the old New York Yak. Politics? Besboll? The Gospel According to Henry David Thoreau? I didn't know and never cared less than on that day. They'd been there when I went up with my office supplies, and were still there when a far less carefree Scott Staley came back down. A Scott Staley who had discovered a small but noticeable hole in the column of reality. Just the two of them being there was enough for me. I walked up and held my right hand, the one with the sunglasses in it, out to Pedro.

"What would you call these?" I asked, not bothering to excuse myself or anything, just butting in headfirst.

He gave me a considering stare that said, "I am surprised at your rudeness, Mr. Staley, truly I am," then looked down at my hand. For a long moment he said nothing, and a horrible idea took possession of me: he saw nothing because there was nothing to see. Only my hand outstretched, as if this were Turnabout Tuesday and I expected *him* to tip *me*. My hand was empty. Sure it was, had to be, because Sonja D'Amico's sunglasses no longer existed. Sonja's joke shades were a long time gone.

"I call them sunglasses, Mr. Staley," Pedro said at last. "What else would I call them? Or is this some sort of trick question?"

Rafe the FedEx man, clearly more interested, took them from me. The relief of seeing him holding the sunglasses and looking at them, almost *studying* them, was like having someone scratch that exact place between your shoulder blades that itches. He stepped out from beneath the awning and held them up to the day, making a sun-star flash off each of the heart-shaped lenses.

"They're like the ones the little girl wore in that porno movie with Jeremy Irons," he said at last.

I had to grin in spite of my distress. In New York, even the deliverymen are film critics. It's one of the things to love about the place.

"That's right, *Lolita*," I said, taking the glasses back. "Only the heart-shaped sunglasses were in the version Stanley Kubrick directed. Back when Jeremy Irons was still nothing but a putter." That one hardly made sense (even to me), but I didn't give Shit One. Once again I was feeling giddy . . . but not in a good way. Not this time.

"Who played the pervo in that one?" Rafe asked.

I shook my head. "I'll be damned if I can remember right now."

"If you don't mind me saying," Pedro said, "you look rather pale, Mr. Staley. Are you coming down with something? The flu, perhaps?"

No, that was my sister, I thought of saying. *The day I came within about twenty seconds of getting caught masturbating into her panties while I looked at a picture of Miss April.* But I hadn't been caught. Not then, not on 9/11, either. Fooled ya, beat the clock again. I couldn't speak for Warren Anderson, who told me in the Blarney Stone that he'd stopped on the third floor that morning to talk about the Yankees with a friend, but not getting caught had become quite a specialty of mine.

"I'm all right," I told Pedro, and while that wasn't true, knowing I wasn't the only one who saw Sonja's joke shades as a thing that actually existed in the world made me feel better, at least. If the sunglasses were in the world, probably Cleve Farrell's Hillerich & Bradsby was, too.

"Are those *the* glasses?" Rafe suddenly asked in a respectful, ready-to-be-awestruck voice. "The ones from the first *Lolita*?"

"Nope," I said, folding the bows behind the heart-shaped lenses, and as I did, the name of the girl in the Kubrick version of the film came to me: Sue Lyon. I still couldn't remember who played the pervo. "Just a knock-off."

"Is there something special about them?" Rafe asked. "Is that why you came rushing down here?"

"I don't know," I said. "Someone left them behind in my apartment."

I went upstairs before they could ask any more questions and looked around, hoping there was nothing else. But there was. In addition to the sunglasses and the baseball bat with CLAIMS ADJUSTOR burned into the side, there was a Howie's Laff-Riot Farting Cushion, a conch shell, a steel penny suspended in a Lucite cube, and a ceramic mushroom (red with white spots) that came with a ceramic Alice sitting on top of it. The Farting Cushion had belonged to Jimmy Eagleton and got a certain amount of play every year at the Christmas party. The ceramic Alice had been on Maureen Hannon's desk—a gift from her granddaughter, she'd told me once. Maureen had the most beautiful white hair, which she wore long, to her waist. You rarely see that in a business situation, but she'd been with the company for almost forty years and felt she could wear her hair any way she liked. I remembered both the conch shell and the steel penny, but not in whose cubicles (or offices) they had been. It might come to me; it might not. There had been lots of cubicles (and offices) at Light and Bell, Insurers.

The shell, the mushroom, and the Lucite cube were on the coffee table in my living room, gathered in a neat pile. The Farting Cushion was—quite rightly, I thought—lying on top of my toilet tank, beside the current issue of Spenck's Rural Insurance Newsletter. Rural insurance used to be my specialty, as I think I told you. I knew all the odds.

What were the odds on this?

When something goes wrong in your life and you need to talk about it, I think that the first impulse for most people is to call a family member. This wasn't much of an option for me. My father put an egg in his shoe and beat it when I was two and my sister was four. My mother, no quitter she, hit the ground running and raised the two of us, managing a mail-order clearinghouse out of our home while she did so. I believe this was a business she actually created, and she made an adequate living at it (only the first year was really scary, she told me later). She smoked like a chimney, however, and died of lung cancer at the age of forty-eight, six or eight years before the Internet might have made her a dotcom millionaire.

My sister Peg was currently living in Cleveland, where she had embraced Mary Kay cosmetics, the Indians, and fundamentalist Christianity, not necessarily in that order. If I called and told Peg about the things I'd found in my apartment, she would suggest I get down on my knees and ask Jesus to come into my life. Rightly or wrongly, I did not feel Jesus could help me with my current problem.

I was equipped with the standard number of aunts, uncles, and cousins, but most lived west of the Mississippi, and I hadn't seen any of them in years. The Killians (my mother's side of the family) have never been a reuning bunch. A card on one's birthday and at Christmas were considered sufficient to fulfill all familial obligations. A card on Valentine's Day or at Easter was a bonus. I called my sister on Christmas or she called me, we muttered the standard crap about getting together "sometime soon," and hung up with what I imagine was mutual relief.

The next option when in trouble would

probably be to invite a good friend out for a drink, explain the situation, and then ask for advice. But I was a shy boy who grew into a shy man, and in my current research job I work alone (out of preference) and thus have no colleagues apt to mature into friends. I made a few in my last job—Sonja and Cleve Farrell, to name two—but they're dead, of course.

I reasoned that if you don't have a friend you can talk to, the next-best thing would be to rent one. I could certainly afford a little therapy, and it seemed to me that a few sessions on some psychiatrist's couch (four might do the trick) would be enough for me to explain what had happened and to articulate how it made me feel. How much could four sessions set me back? Six hundred dollars? Maybe eight? That seemed a fair price for a little relief. And I thought there might be a bonus. A disinterested outsider might be able to see some simple and reasonable explanation I was just missing. To my mind the locked door between my apartment and the outside world seemed to do away with most of those, but it was *my* mind, after all; wasn't that the point? And perhaps the problem?

I had it all mapped out. During the first session I'd explain what had happened. When I came to the second one, I'd bring the items in question—sunglasses, Lucite cube, conch shell, baseball bat, ceramic mushroom, the ever-popular Farting Cushion. A little show and tell, just like in grammar school. That left two more during which my rent-a-pal and I could figure out the cause of this disturbing tilt in the axis of my life and set things straight again.

A single afternoon spent riffling the Yellow Pages and dialing the telephone was enough to prove to me that the idea of psychiatry was unworkable in fact, no matter how good it might be in theory. The closest I came to an actual appointment was a receptionist who told me that Dr. Jauss might be able to work me in the following January. She intimated even that would take some inspired shoehorning. The others held out no hope whatsoever. I tried half a dozen therapists in Newark and four in White Plains, even a hypnotist in Queens, with the same result. Mohammed Atta and his Suicide Patrol might have been very bery-bery bad for the city of New York (not to mention for the in-SHOO-rance business), but it was clear to me from that single fruitless afternoon on the telephone that they had been a boon to the psychiatric profession, much as the psychiatrists themselves might wish otherwise. If you wanted to lie on some professional's couch in the summer of 2002, you had to take a number and wait in line.

I could sleep with those things in my apartment, but not well. They whispered to me. I lay awake in my bed, sometimes until two, thinking about Maureen Hannon, who felt she had reached an age (not to mention a level of indispensability) at which she could wear her amazingly long hair any way she damn well liked. Or I'd recall the various people who'd gone running around at the Christmas party, waving Jimmy Eagleton's famous Farting Cushion. It was, as I may have said, a great favorite once people got two or three drinks closer to New Year's. I remembered Bruce Mason asking me if it didn't look like an enema bag for elfs—"elfs," he said—and by a process of association remembered that the conch shell had been his. Of course. Bruce Mason, Lord of the Flies. And a step further down the associative food chain I found the name and face of James Mason, who had played Humbert Humbert back when Jeremy Irons was still just a putter. The mind is a wily monkey; sometime him take-a de banana, sometime him don't. Which is why I'd brought the sunglasses downstairs, although I'd been aware of no deductive process at the time. I'd only wanted confirmation. There's a George Seferis poem that asks, *Are these the voices of our dead friends, or is it just the gramophone?* Sometimes it's a good question, one you have to ask someone else. Or . . . listen to this.

Once, in the late eighties, near the end of a bitter two-year romance with alcohol, I woke up in my study after dozing off at my desk in the middle of the night. I staggered off to my bedroom, where, as I reached for the light switch, I saw someone moving around. I flashed on the idea (the near *certainty*) of a junkie burglar with a cheap pawnshop .32 in his trembling hand, and my heart almost came out of my chest. I turned on the light with one hand and was grabbing for something heavy off the top of my bureau with the other—anything, even the silver frame holding the picture of my mother, would have done—when I saw the prowler was me. I was staring wild-eyed back at myself from the mirror on the other side of the room, my shirt half-untucked and my hair standing up in the back. I was disgusted with myself, but I was also relieved.

I wanted this to be like that. I wanted it to be the mirror, the gramophone, even someone playing a nasty practical joke (maybe someone who knew why I hadn't been at the office on that day in September). But I knew it was none of those things. The Farting Cushion was there, an actual guest in my apartment. I could run my thumb over the buckles on Alice's ceramic shoes, slide my finger down the part in her yellow ceramic hair. I could read the date on the penny inside the Lucite cube.

Bruce Mason, alias Conch Man, alias Lord of the Flies, took his big pink shell to the company shindig at Jones Beach one July and blew it, summoning people to a jolly picnic lunch of hotdogs and hamburgers. Then he tried to show Freddy Lounds how to do it. The best Freddy had been able to muster was a series of weak honking sounds like ... well, like Jimmy Eagleton's Farting Cushion. Around and around it goes. Ultimately, every associative chain forms a necklace.

In late September I had a brainstorm, one of those ideas so simple you can't believe you didn't think of it sooner. Why was I holding onto this unwelcome crap, anyway? Why not just get rid of it? It wasn't as if the items were in trust; the people who owned them weren't going to come back at some later date and ask for them to be returned. The last time I'd seen Cleve Farrell's face it had been on a poster, and the last of those had been torn down by November of '01. The general (if unspoken) feeling was that such homemade homages were bumming out the tourists, who'd begun to creep back to Fun City. What had happened was horrible, most New Yorkers opined, but America was still here and Matthew Broderick would only be in *The Producers* for so long.

I'd gotten Chinese that night, from a

place I like two blocks over. My plan was to eat it as I usually ate my evening meal, watching Chuck Scarborough explain the world to me. I was turning on the television when the epiphany came. They *weren't* in trust, these unwelcome souvenirs of the last safe day, nor were they evidence. There had been a crime, yes—everyone agreed to that—but the perpetrators were dead and the ones who'd set them on their crazy course were on the run. There might be trials at some future date, but Scott Staley would never be called to the stand, and Jimmy Eagleton's Farting Cushion would never be marked Exhibit A.

I left my General Tso's chicken sitting on the kitchen counter with the cover still on the aluminum dish, got a laundry bag from the shelf above my seldom-used washing machine, put the things into it (sacking them up, I couldn't believe how light they were, or how long I'd waited to do such a simple thing), and rode down in the elevator with the bag sitting between my feet. I walked to the corner of 75th and Park, looked around to make sure I wasn't being watched (God knows why I felt so furtive, but I did), then put litter in its place. I took one look back over my shoulder as I walked away. The handle of the bat poked out of the basket invitingly. Someone would come along and take it, I had no doubt. Probably before Chuck Scarborough gave way to John Seigenthaler or whoever else was sitting in for Tom Brokaw that evening.

On my way back to my apartment, I stopped at Fun Choy for a fresh order of General Tso's. "Last one no good?" asked Rose Ming, at the cash register. She spoke with some concern. "You tell why."

"No, the last one was fine," I said. "Tonight I just felt like two."

She laughed as though this were the funniest thing she'd ever heard, and I laughed, too. Hard. The kind of laughter that goes well beyond giddy. I couldn't remember the last time I'd laughed like that, so loudly and so naturally. Certainly not since Light and Bell, Insurers, fell into West Street.

I rode the elevator up to my floor and walked the twelve steps to 4-B. I felt the way seriously ill people must when they awaken one day, assess themselves by the sane light of morning, and discover that the fever has broken. I tucked my takeout bag under my left arm (an awkward maneuver but work-able in the short run) and then unlocked my door. I turned on the light. There, on the table where I leave bills that need to be paid, claim checks, and overdue-book notices, were Sonja D'Amico's joke sunglasses, the ones with the red frames and the heart-shaped Lolita lenses. Sonja D'Amico who had, according to Warren Anderson (who was, so far as I knew, the only other surviving employee of Light and Bell's home office), jumped from the one hundred and tenth floor of the stricken building.

He claimed to have seen a photo that caught her as she dropped, Sonja with her hands placed primly on her skirt to keep it from skating up her thighs, her hair stand-ing up against the smoke and blue of that day's sky, the tips of her shoes pointed down. The description made me think of "Falling," the poem James Dickey wrote about the stew-ardess who tries to aim the plummeting stone of her body for water, as if she could come up smiling, shaking beads of water from her hair and asking for a Coca-Cola.

"I vomited," Warren told me that day in the Blarney Stone. "I never want to look at a picture like that again, Scott, but I know I'll never forget it. You could see her face, and I think she believed that somehow . . . yeah, that somehow she was going to be all right."

I've never screamed as an adult, but I almost did so when I looked from Sonja's sunglasses to Cleve Farrell's CLAIMS ADJUSTOR, the latter once more leaning nonchalantly in the corner by the entry to the living room. Some part of my mind must have remembered that the door to the hallway was open and both of my fourth-floor neighbors would hear me if I did scream; then, as the saying is, I would have some 'splainin to do.

I clapped my hand over my mouth to hold it in. The bag with the General Tso's chicken inside fell to the hardwood floor of the foyer and split open. I could barely bring myself to look at the resulting mess. Those dark chunks of cooked meat could have been anything.

I plopped into the single chair I keep in the foyer and put my face in my hands. I didn't scream and I didn't cry, and after a while I was able to clean up the mess. My mind kept trying to go toward the things that had beaten me back from the corner of 75th and Park, but I wouldn't let it. Each time it tried to lunge in that direction, I grabbed its leash and forced it away again.

That night, lying in bed, I listened to conversations. First the things talked (in low voices), and then the people who had owned the things replied (in slightly louder ones). Sometimes they talked about the picnic at Jones Beach—the coconut odor of suntan lotion and Lou Bega singing "Mambo No. 5" over and over from Misha Bryzinski's boom box. Or they talked about Frisbees sailing under the sky while dogs chased them. Sometimes they discussed children puddling along the wet sand with the seats of their shorts and their bathing suits sagging. Mothers in swimsuits ordered from the Lands' End catalogue walking beside them with white gloop on their noses. How many of the kids that day had lost a guardian Mom or a Frisbee-throwing Dad? Man, that was a math problem I didn't want to do. But the voices I heard in my apartment *did* want to do it. They did it over and over.

I remembered Bruce Mason blowing his

conch shell and proclaiming himself the Lord of the Flies. I remembered Maureen Hannon once telling me (not at Jones Beach, not this conversation) that *Alice in Wonderland* was the first psychedelic novel. Jimmy Eagleton telling me one afternoon that his son had a learning disability to go along with his stutter, two for the price of one, and the kid was going to need a tutor in math and another one in French if he was going to get out of high school in the foreseeable future. "Before he's eligible for the AARP discount on textbooks" was how Jimmy had put it. His cheeks pale and a bit stubbly in the long afternoon light, as if that morning the razor had been dull.

I'd been drifting toward sleep, but this last one brought me fully awake again with a start, because I realized the conversation must have taken place not long before September Eleventh. Maybe only days. Perhaps even the Friday before, which would make it the last day I'd ever seen Jimmy alive. And the l'il putter with the stutter and the learning disability: had his name actually been Jeremy, as in Jeremy Irons? Surely not, surely that was just my mind (sometime him take-a de banana) playing its little games, but it had been *close* to that, by God. Jason, maybe. Or Justin. In the wee hours everything grows, and I remember thinking that if the kid's name *did* turn out to be Jeremy, I'd probably go crazy. Straw that broke the camel's back, baby.

Around three in the morning I remembered who had owned the Lucite cube with the steel penny in it: Roland Abelson, in Liability. He called it his retirement fund. It was Roland who had a habit of saying "Lucy, you got some 'splainin to do." One night in the fall of '01, I had seen his widow on the six o'clock news. I had talked with her at one of the company picnics (very likely the one at Jones Beach) and thought then that she was pretty, but widowhood had refined that prettiness, winnowed it into severe beauty. On the news report she kept referring to her husband as "missing." She would not call him "dead." And if he *was* alive—if he ever turned up—he would have some 'splainin to do. You bet. But of course, so would she. A woman who has gone from pretty to beautiful as the result of a mass murder would certainly have some 'splainin to do.

Lying in bed and thinking of this stuff—remembering the crash of the surf at Jones Beach and the Frisbees flying under the sky—filled me with an awful sadness that finally emptied in tears. But I have to admit it was a learning experience. That was the night I came to understand that *things*—even little ones, like a penny in a Lucite cube—can get heavier as time passes. But because it's a weight of the mind, there's no mathematical formula for it, like the ones you can find in an insurance company's Blue Books, where the rate on your whole life policy goes up x if you smoke and coverage on your crops goes up y if your farm's in a tornado zone. You see what I'm saying?

It's a weight of the mind.

The following morning I gathered up all the items again, and found a seventh, this one under the couch. The guy in the cubicle next to mine, Misha Bryzinski, had kept a small pair of Punch and Judy dolls on his desk. The one I spied under my sofa with my little eye was Punch. Judy was nowhere to be found, but Punch was enough for me. Those black eyes, staring out from amid the ghost bunnies, gave me a terrible sinking feeling of dismay. I fished the doll out, hating the streak of dust it left behind. A thing that leaves a trail is a real thing, a thing with weight. No question about it.

I put Punch and all the other stuff in the little utility closet just off the kitchenette, and there they stayed. At first I wasn't sure they would, but they did.

My mother once told me that if a man wiped his ass and saw blood on the toilet tissue, his response would be to shit in the dark for the next thirty days and hope for the best. She used this example to illustrate her belief that the cornerstone of male philosophy was "If you ignore it, maybe it'll go away."

I ignored the things I'd found in my apartment, I hoped for the best, and things actually got a little better. I rarely heard those voices whispering in the utility closet (except late at night), although I was more and more apt to take my research chores out of the house. By the middle of November, I was spending most of my days in the New York

Public Library. I'm sure the lions got used to seeing me there with my PowerBook.

Then, just before Thanksgiving, I happened to be going out of my building one day and met Paula Robeson, the maiden fair whom I'd rescued by pushing the reset button on her air conditioner, coming in.

With absolutely no forethought whatsoever—if I'd had time to think about it, I'm convinced I never would have said a word—I asked her if I could buy her lunch and talk to her about something.

"The fact is," I said, "I have a problem. Maybe you could push my reset button."

We were in the lobby. Pedro the doorman was sitting in the corner, reading the *Post* (and listening to every word, I have no doubt—to Pedro, his tenants were the world's most interesting daytime drama). She gave me a smile both pleasant and nervous. "I guess I owe you one," she said, "but . . . you know I'm married, don't you?"

"Yes," I said, not adding that she'd shaken with me wrong-handed so I could hardly fail to notice the ring.

She nodded. "Sure, you must've seen us together at least a couple of times, but he was in Europe when I had all that trouble with the air conditioner, and he's in Europe now. Edward, that's his name. Over the last two years he's been in Europe more than he's here, and although I don't like it, I'm very married in spite of it." Then, as a kind of afterthought, she added: "Edward is in import-export."

I used to be in insurance, but then one day the company exploded, I thought of saying. Came *close* to saying, actually. In the end, I managed something a little more sane.

"I don't want a date, Ms. Robeson," No more than I wanted to be on a first-name basis with her, and was that a wink of disappointment I saw in her eyes? By God, I thought it was. But at least it convinced her. I was still *safe.*

She put her hands on her hips and looked at me with mock exasperation. Or maybe not so mock. "Then what *do* you want?"

"Just someone to talk to. I tried several shrinks, but they're . . . busy."

"*All* of them?"

"It would appear so."

"If you're having problems with your sex life or feeling the urge to race around town killing men in turbans, I don't want to know about it."

"It's nothing like that. I'm not going to make you blush, I promise." Which wasn't quite the same as saying *I promise not to shock you* or *You won't think I'm crazy.* "Just lunch and a little advice, that's all I'm asking. What do you say?"

I was surprised—almost flabbergasted—by my own persuasiveness. If I'd planned the conversation in advance, I almost certainly would have blown the whole deal. I suppose she was curious, and I'm sure she heard a degree of sincerity in my voice. She may also have surmised that if I was the sort of man who liked to try his hand picking up women, I would have had a go on that day in August when I'd actually been alone with her in her apartment, the elusive Edward in France or Germany. And I have to wonder how much actual desperation she saw in my face.

In any case, she agreed to have lunch with me at Donald's Grill down the street on Friday. Donald's may be the least romantic restaurant in all of Manhattan—good food, fluorescent lights, waiters who make it clear they'd like you to hurry. She did so with the air of a woman paying an overdue debt about which she's nearly forgotten. This was not exactly flattering, but it was good enough for me. Noon would be fine for her, she said. If I'd meet her in the lobby, we could walk down there together. I told her that would be fine for me, too.

That night was a good one for me. I went to sleep almost immediately, and there were no dreams of Sonja D'Amico going down beside the burning building with her hands on her thighs, like a stewardess looking for water.

As we strolled down 86th Street the following day, I asked Paula where she'd been when she heard.

"San Francisco," she said. "Fast asleep in a Wradling Hotel suite with Edward beside me, undoubtedly snoring as usual. I was coming back here on September twelfth and Edward was going on to Los Angeles for meetings. The hotel management actually rang the fire alarm."

"That must have scared the hell out of you."

"It did, although my first thought wasn't

fire but earthquake. Then this disembodied voice came through the speakers, telling us that there was no fire in the hotel, but a hell of a big one in New York."

"Jesus."

"Hearing it like that, in bed in a strange room . . . hearing it come down from the ceiling like the voice of God . . ." She shook her head. Her lips were pressed so tightly together that her lipstick almost disappeared. "That was very frightening. I suppose I understand the urge to pass on news like that, and immediately, but I still haven't entirely forgiven the management of the Wradling for doing it that way. I don't think I'll be staying there again."

"Did your husband go on to his meetings?"

"They were canceled. I imagine a lot of meetings were canceled that day. We stayed in bed with the TV on until the sun came up, trying to get our heads around it. Do you know what I mean?"

"Yes."

"We talked about who might have been there that we knew. I suppose we weren't the only ones doing that, either."

"Did you come up with anyone?"

"A broker from Shearson Lehman and the assistant manager of the Borders book store in the mall," she said. "One of them was all right. One of them . . . well, you know, one of them wasn't. What about you?"

So I didn't have to sneak up on it, after all. We weren't even at the restaurant yet and here it was.

"*I* would have been there," I said. "I *should* have been there. It's where I worked. In an insurance company on the hundred and tenth floor."

She stopped dead on the sidewalk, looking up at me, eyes wide. I suppose to the people who had to veer around us, we must have looked like lovers. "Scott, *no!*"

"Scott, yes," I said. And finally told someone about how I woke up on September eleventh expecting to do all the things I usually did on weekdays, from the cup of black coffee while I shaved all the way to the cup of cocoa in front of the midnight news summary on Channel Thirteen. A day like any other day, that was what I had in mind. I think that is what Americans had come to expect as their right. Well, guess what? That's an airplane! Flying into the side of a skyscraper! Ha-ha, asshole, the joke's on you, and half the goddam world's laughing!

I told her about looking out my apartment window and seeing the seven A.M. sky was perfectly cloudless, the sort of blue so deep you think you can almost see through it to the stars beyond. Then I told her about the voice. I think everyone has various voices in their heads and we get used to them. When I was sixteen, one of mine spoke up and suggested it might be quite a kick to masturbate into a pair of my sister's underpants. *She has about a thousand pairs and surely won't miss one, y'all,* the voice opined. (I did not tell Paula Robeson about this particular adolescent adventure.) I'd have to call that the voice of utter irresponsibility, more familiarly known as Mr. Yow, Git Down.

"Mr. Yow, Git Down?" Paula asked doubtfully.

"In honor of James Brown, the King of Soul."

"If you say so."

Mr. Yow, Git Down had had less and less to say to me, especially since I'd pretty much given up drinking, and on that day he awoke from his doze just long enough to speak a dozen words, but they were life-changers. Life-*savers.*

The first five (that's me, sitting on the edge of the bed): *Yow, call in sick, y'all!* The next seven (that's me, plodding toward the shower and scratching my left buttock as I go): *Yow, spend the day in Central Park!* There was no premonition involved. It was clearly Mr. Yow, Git Down, not the voice of God. It was just a version of my very own voice (as they all are), in other words, telling me to play hooky. *Do a little suffin fo' yo'self, Gre't God!* The last time I could recall hearing this version of my voice, the subject had been a karaoke contest at a bar on Amsterdam Avenue: *Yow, sing along wit' Neil Diamond, fool—git up on stage and git ya bad self down!*

"I guess I know what you mean," she said, smiling a little.

"Do you?"

"Well . . . I once took off my shirt in a Key West bar and won ten dollars dancing to 'Honky Tonk Women.'" She paused. "Edward doesn't know, and if you ever tell him, I'll be forced to stab you in the eye with one of his tie tacks."

"Yow, you go, girl," I said, and her smile became a rather wistful grin. It made her look younger. I thought this had a chance of working.

We walked into Donald's. There was a cardboard turkey on the door, cardboard Pilgrims on the green tile wall above the steam table.

"I listened to Mr. Yow, Git Down and I'm here," I said. "But some other things are here, too, and he can't help with them. They're things I can't seem to get rid of. Those are what I want to talk to you about."

"Let me repeat that I'm no shrink," she said, and with more than a trace of uneasiness. The grin was gone. "I majored in German and minored in European history."

You and your husband must have a lot to talk about, I thought. What I said out loud was that it didn't have to be her, necessarily, just someone.

"All right. Just as long as you know."

A waiter took our drink orders, decaf for her, regular for me. Once he went away she asked me what things I was talking about.

"This is one of them." From my pocket I withdrew the Lucite cube with the steel penny suspended inside it and put it on the table. Then I told her about the other things, and to whom they had belonged. Cleve "Besboll been bery-bery good to me" Farrell. Maureen Hannon, who wore her hair long to her waist as a sign of her corporate indispensability. Jimmy Eagleton, who had a divine nose for phony accident claims, a son with learning disabilities, and a Farting Cushion he kept safely tucked away in his desk until the Christmas party rolled around each year. Sonja D'Amico, Light and Bell's best accountant, who had gotten the Lolita sunglasses as a bitter divorce present from her first husband. Bruce "Lord of the Flies" Mason, who would always stand shirtless in my mind's eye, blowing his conch on Jones Beach while the waves rolled up and expired around his bare feet. Last of all, Misha Bryzinski, with whom I'd gone to at least a dozen Mets games. I told her about putting everything but Misha's Punch doll in a trash basket on the corner of Park and 75th, and how they had beaten me back to my apartment, possibly because I had stopped for a second order of General Tso's chicken. During all of this, the Lucite cube stood on the table between us. We managed to eat at least some of our meal in spite of his stern profile.

When I was finished talking, I felt better than I'd dared to hope. But there was a silence from her side of the table that felt terribly heavy.

"So," I said, to break it. "What do you think?"

She took a moment to consider that, and I didn't blame her. "I think that we're not the strangers we were," she said finally, "and making a new friend is never a bad thing. I think I'm glad I know about Mr. Yow, Git Down and that I told you what I did."

"I am, too." And it was true.

"Now may I ask you two questions?"

"Of course."

"How much of what they call 'survivor guilt' are you feeling?"

"I thought you said you weren't a shrink."

"I'm not, but I read the magazines and have even been known to watch *Oprah*. That my husband *does* know, although I prefer not to rub his nose in it. So . . . how much, Scott?"

I considered the question. It was a good one—and, of course, it was one I'd asked myself on more than one of those sleepless nights. "Quite a lot," I said. "Also, quite a lot of relief, I won't lie about that. If Mr. Yow, Git Down was a real person, he'd never have to pick up another restaurant tab. Not when I was with him, at least." I paused. "Does that shock you?"

She reached across the table and briefly touched my hand. "Not even a little."

Hearing her say that made me feel better than I would have believed. I gave her hand a brief squeeze and then let it go. "What's your other question?"

"How important to you is it that I believe your story about these things coming back?"

I thought this was an excellent question, even though the Lucite cube was right there next to the sugar bowl. Such items are not exactly rare, after all. And I thought that if she *had* majored in psychology rather than German, she probably would have done fine.

"Not as important as I thought an hour ago," I said. "Just telling it has been a help."

She nodded and smiled. "Good. Now here's my best guess: someone is very likely playing a game with you. Not a nice one."

"Trickin' on me," I said. I tried not to show it, but I'd rarely been so disappointed. Maybe a layer of disbelief settles over people in certain circumstances, protecting them. Or maybe—probably—I hadn't conveyed my own sense that this thing was just . . . happening. *Still* happening. The way avalanches do.

"Trickin' on you," she agreed, and then: "But you don't believe it."

More points for perception. I nodded. "I locked the door when I went out, and it was locked when I came back from Staples. I heard the clunk the tumblers make when they turn. They're loud. You can't miss them."

"Still . . . survivor guilt is a funny thing. And powerful, at least according to the magazines."

"This . . ." *This isn't survivor guilt* was what I meant to say, but it would have been the wrong thing. I had a fighting chance to make a new friend here, and having a new friend would be good, no matter how the rest of this came out. So I amended it. "I don't think this is survivor guilt." I pointed to the Lucite cube. "It's right there, isn't it? Like Sonja's sunglasses. You see it. I do, too. I suppose I could have bought it myself, but . . ." I shrugged, trying to convey what we both surely knew: *anything* is possible.

"I don't think you did that. But neither can I accept the idea that a trapdoor opened between reality and the twilight zone and these things fell out."

Yes, that was the problem. For Paula the idea that the Lucite cube and the other things which had appeared in my apartment had some supernatural origin was automatically off-limits, no matter how much the facts might seem to support the idea. What I needed to do was to decide if I needed to argue the point more than I needed to make a friend.

I decided I did not.

"All right," I said. I caught the waiter's eye and made a check-writing gesture in the air. "I can accept your inability to accept."

"Can you?" she asked, looking at me closely.

"Yes." And I thought it was true. "If, that is, we could have a cup of coffee from time to time. Or just say hi in the lobby."

"Absolutely." But she sounded absent, not really in the conversation. She was looking at the Lucite cube with the steel penny inside it. Then she looked up at me. I could almost see a lightbulb appearing over her head, like in a cartoon. She reached out and grasped the cube with one hand. I could never convey the depth of the dread I felt when she did that, but what could I say? We were New Yorkers in a clean, well-lighted place. For her part, she'd already laid down the ground rules, and they pretty firmly excluded the supernatural. The supernatural was out of bounds. Anything hit there was a do-over.

And there was a light in Paula's eyes. One that suggested Ms. Yow, Git Down was in the house, and I know from personal experience that's a hard voice to resist.

"Give it to me," she proposed, smiling into my eyes. When she did that I could see—for the first time, really—that she was sexy as well as pretty.

"Why?" As if I didn't know.

"Call it my fee for listening to your story."

"I don't know if that's such a good—"

"It is, though," she said. She was warming to her own inspiration, and when people do that, they rarely take no for an answer. "It's a *great* idea. I'll make sure this piece of memorabilia at least doesn't come back to you, wagging its tail behind it. We've got a safe in the apartment." She made a charming little pantomime gesture of shutting a safe door, twirling the combination, and then throwing the key back over her shoulder.

"All right," I said. "It's my gift to you." And I felt something that might have been mean-spirited gladness. Call it the voice of Mr. Yow, You'll Find Out. Apparently just getting it off my chest wasn't enough, after all. She hadn't believed me, and at least part of me *did* want to be believed and resented Paula for not getting what it wanted. That part knew that letting her take the Lucite cube was an absolutely terrible idea, but was glad to see her tuck it away in her purse, just the same.

"There," she said briskly. "Mama say bye-bye, make all gone. Maybe when it doesn't come back in a week—or two, I guess it all depends on how stubborn your subconscious wants to be—you can start giving the rest of the things away." And her saying that was her real gift to me that day, although I didn't know it then.

"Maybe so," I said, and smiled. Big smile for the new friend. Big smile for pretty Mama. All the time thinking, You'll find out. Yow.

She did.

Three nights later, while I was watching Chuck Scarborough explain the city's latest transit woes on the six o'clock news, my doorbell rang. Since no one had been announced, I assumed it was a package, maybe even Rafe with something from FedEx. I opened the door and there stood Paula Robeson.

This was not the woman with whom I'd had lunch. Call this version of Paula Ms. Yow, Ain't That Chemotherapy *Nasty*. She was wearing a little lipstick but nothing else in the way of makeup, and her complexion was a sickly shade of yellow-white. There were dark brownish-purple arcs under her eyes. She might have given her hair a token swipe with the brush before coming down from the fifth floor, but it hadn't done much good. It looked like straw and stuck out on either side of her head in a way that would have been comic-strip funny under other circumstances. She was holding the Lucite cube up in front of her breasts, allowing me to note that the well-kept nails on that hand were gone. She'd chewed them away, right down to the quick. And my first thought, God help me, was *yep, she found out.*

She held it out to me. "Take it back," she said.

I did so without a word.

"His name was Roland Abelson," she said. "Wasn't it?"

"Yes."

"He had red hair."

"Yes."

"Not married but paying child support to a woman in Rahway."

I hadn't known that—didn't believe *anyone* at Light and Bell had known that—but I nodded again, and not just to keep her rolling. I was sure she was right. "What was her name, Paula?" Not knowing why I was asking, not yet, just knowing I had to know.

"Tonya Gregson." It was as if she was in a trance. There was something in her eyes, though, something so terrible I could hardly stand to look at it. Nevertheless, I stored the name away. *Tonya Gregson, Rahway.* And then, like some guy doing stockroom inventory: *One Lucite cube with penny inside.*

"He tried to crawl under his desk, did you know that? No, I can see you didn't. His hair was on fire and he was crying. Because in that instant he understood he was never going to own a catamaran or even mow his lawn again." She reached out and put a hand on my cheek, a gesture so intimate it would have been shocking had her hand not been so cold. "At the end, he would have given every cent he had, and every stock option he held, just to be able to mow his lawn again. Do you believe that?"

"Yes."

"The place was full of screams, he could smell jet fuel, and *he understood it was his dying hour.* Do you understand that? Do you understand the *enormity* of that?"

I nodded. I couldn't speak. You could have put a gun to my head and I still wouldn't have been able to speak.

"The politicians talk about memorials and courage and wars to end terrorism, but burning hair is apolitical." She bared her teeth in an unspeakable grin. A moment later it was gone. "He was trying to crawl under his desk with his hair on fire. There was a plastic thing under his desk, a what-do-you-call-it—"

"Mat—"

"Yes, a mat, a plastic mat, and his hands

were on that and he could feel the ridges in the plastic and smell his own burning hair. Do you understand that?"

I nodded. I started to cry. It was Roland Abelson we were talking about, this guy I used to work with. He was in Liability and I didn't know him very well. To say hi to is all; how was I supposed to know he had a kid in Rahway? And if I hadn't played hooky that day, my hair probably would have burned, too. I'd never really understood that before.

"I don't want to see you again," she said. She flashed her gruesome grin once more, but now she was crying, too. "I don't care about your problems. I don't care about any of the shit you found. We're quits. From now on you leave me alone." She started to turn away, then turned back. She said: "They did it in the name of God, but there is no God. If there was a God, Mr. Staley, He would have struck all eighteen of them dead in their boarding lounges with their boarding passes in their hands, but no God did. They called for passengers to get on and those fucks just got on."

I watched her walk back to the elevator. Her back was very stiff. Her hair stuck out on either side of her head, making her look like a girl in a Sunday funnies cartoon. She didn't want to see me anymore, and I didn't blame her. I closed the door and looked at the steel Abe Lincoln in the Lucite cube. I looked at him for quite a long time. I thought about how the hair of his beard would have smelled if U.S. Grant had stuck one of his everlasting cigars in it. That unpleasant frying aroma. On TV, someone was saying that there was a mattress blowout going on at Sleepy's. After that, Len Berman came on and talked about the Jets.

That night I woke up at two in the morning, listening to the voices whisper. I hadn't had any dreams or visions of the people who owned the objects, hadn't seen anyone with their hair on fire or jumping from the windows to escape the burning jet fuel, but why would I? I knew who they were, and the things they left behind had been left for me. Letting Paula Robeson take the Lucite cube had been wrong, but only because she was the wrong person.

And speaking of Paula, one of the voices

was hers. *You can start giving the rest of the things away,* it said. And it said, *I guess it all depends on how stubborn your subconscious wants to be.*

I lay back down and after a while I was able to go to sleep. I dreamed I was in Central Park, feeding the ducks, when all at once there was a loud noise like a sonic boom and smoke filled the sky. In my dream, the smoke smelled like burning hair.

I thought about Tonya Gregson in Rahway—Tonya and the child who might or might not have Roland Abelson's eyes—and thought I'd have to work up to that one. I decided to start with Bruce Mason's widow.

I took the train to Dobbs Ferry and called a taxi from the station. The cabbie took me to a Cape Cod house on a residential street. I gave him some money, told him to wait—I wouldn't be long—and rang the doorbell. I had a box under one arm. It looked like the kind that contains a bakery cake.

I only had to ring once because I'd called ahead and Janice Mason was expecting me. I had my story carefully prepared and told it with some confidence, knowing that the taxi sitting in the driveway, its meter running, would forestall any detailed cross-examination.

On September seventh, I said—the Friday before—I had tried to blow a note from the conch Bruce kept on his desk, as I had heard Bruce himself do at the Jones Beach picnic. (Janice, Mrs. Lord of the Flies, nodding; she had been there, of course.) Well, I said, to make a long story short, I had persuaded Bruce to let me have the conch shell over the weekend so I could practice. Then, on Tuesday morning, I'd awakened with a raging sinus infection and a horrible headache to go with it. (This was a story I had already told several people.) I'd been drinking a cup of tea when I heard the boom and saw the rising smoke. I hadn't thought of the conch shell again until just this week. I'd been cleaning out my little utility closet and by damn, there it was. And I just thought . . . well, it's not much of a keepsake, but I just thought maybe you'd like to . . . you know . . .

Her eyes filled up with tears just as mine had when Paula brought back Roland Abelson's "retirement fund," only these weren't accompanied by the look of fright that I'm sure was on my own face as Paula stood there with her stiff hair sticking out on either side of her head. Janice told me she would be glad to have any keepsake of Bruce.

"I can't get over the way we said good-bye," she said, holding the box in her arms. "He always left very early because he took the train. He kissed me on the cheek and I opened one eye and asked him if he'd bring back a pint of half-and-half. He said he would. That's the last thing he ever said to me. When he asked me to marry him, I felt like Helen of Troy—stupid but absolutely true—and I wish I'd said something better than 'Bring home a pint of half-and-half.' But we'd been married a long time, and it seemed like business as usual that day, and . . . we don't know, do we?"

"No."

"Yes. Any parting could be forever, and we don't know. Thank you, Mr. Staley. For coming out and bringing me this. That was very kind." She smiled a little then. "Do you remember how he stood on the beach with his shirt off and blew it?"

"Yes," I said, and looked at the way she held the box. Later she would sit down and take the shell out and hold it on her lap and cry. I knew that the conch, at least, would never come back to my apartment. It was home.

I returned to the station and caught the train back to New York. The cars were almost empty at that time of day, early afternoon, and I sat by a rain- and dirt-streaked window, looking out at the river and the approaching skyline. On cloudy and rainy days, you almost seem to be creating that skyline out of your own imagination, a piece at a time.

Tomorrow I'd go to Rahway, with the penny in the Lucite cube. Perhaps the child would take it in his or her chubby hand and look at it curiously. In any case, it would be out of my life. I thought the only difficult thing to get rid of would be Jimmy Eagleton's Farting Cushion—I could hardly tell Mrs. Eagleton I'd brought it home for the weekend in order to practice using it, could I? But necessity is the mother of invention, and I was confident that I would eventually think of some halfway plausible story.

It occurred to me that other things might show up, in time. And I'd be lying if I told you I found that possibility entirely unpleasant. When it comes to returning things which people believe have been lost forever, things that have *weight*, there are compensations. Even if they're only little things, like a pair of joke sunglasses or a steel penny in a Lucite cube . . . yeah. I'd have to say there are compensations.

JOHN FARRIS

John Farris began writing fiction in high school. At 22, while he was studying at the University of Missouri, his first major novel, *Harrison High,* was published; it became a bestseller. He has worked in many genres—suspense, horror, mystery—while transcending each through the power of his writing. The *New York Times* noted his talent for "masterfully devious plotting" while reviewing *The Captors. All Heads Turn When the Hunt Goes By* was cited in an essay published in *Horror: 100 Best Books,* which concluded, "The field's most powerful individual voice . . . when John Farris is on high-burn, no one can match the skill with which he puts words together." In the 1990s, he turned exclusively to thrillers, publishing *Dragonfly, Soon She Will Be Gone, Solar Eclipse,* and *Sacrifice,* of which Richard Matheson wrote, "John Farris has once again elevated the terror genre into the realm of literature." Commenting on *Dragonfly,* Ed Gorman said, "*Dragonfly* has style, heart, cunning, terror, irony, suspense, and genuine surprise—and an absolutely fearless look into the souls of people very much like you and me." And *Publishers Weekly* concluded, "(he writes with) a keen knowledge of human nature and a wicked sense of humor." John Farris received the 2001 Bram Stoker Award for Lifetime Achievement from the Horror Writers Association. His latest novel is *Phantom Nights.*

THE RANSOME WOMEN

John Farris

ONE

Echo Halloran first became aware of the Woman in Black during a visit to the Highbridge Museum of Art in Cambridge, Massachusetts. Echo and her boss were dealing that day with the chief curator of the Highbridge, a man named Charles Carwood. The Highbridge was in the process of deacquisitioning, as they say in the trade, a number of paintings, mostly by twentieth-century artists whose stock had remained stable in the fickle art world. The Highbridge was in difficulty with the IRS and Carwood was looking for around thirty million for a group of Representationalists.

Echo's boss was Stefan Konine, director of Gilbard's, the New York auction house. Stefan was a big man, florid as a poached salmon, who lied about his age and played the hay burners for recreation. He wore J. Dege & Sons suits with the aplomb of royalty. He wasn't much interested in Representationalists and preferred to let Echo, who had done her thesis at NYU on the Boquillas School, carry the ball while the paintings were reverently brought, one by one, to their attention in the seventh-floor conference room. The weather outside was blue and clear. Through a nice spread of windows the view to the south included the Charles River.

Echo had worked for Konine for a little over a year. They had established an almost familial rapport. Echo kept busy with her laptop on questions of provenance while Stefan sipped Chablis and regarded each painting with the same dyspeptic expression, as if he were trying to digest a bowling ball he'd had for lunch. His mind was mostly on the trifecta he had working at Belmont, but he was alert to the nuances of each glance Echo sent his way. They were a team. They knew each other's signals.

Carwood said, "And we have this exquisite

David Herrera from the Oppenheim estate, probably the outstanding piece of David's Big Bend Cycle."

Echo smiled as two museum assistants wheeled in the oversize canvas. She was drinking 7Up, not Chablis.

The painting was in the style of Georgia O'Keeffe during her Santa Fe incarnation. Echo looked down at her laptop screen, hit a few keys, looked up again. It was a long stare, as if she were trying to see all the way to the Big Bend Country of Texas. After a couple of minutes Stefan raised a spikey eyebrow. Carwood fidgeted on his settee. His eyes were on Echo. He had done some staring himself, from the moment Echo was introduced to him.

There are beauties who stop traffic and there are beauties who grow obsessively in the hearts of the susceptible; Echo Halloran was one of those. She had a full mane of wraparound dark hair. Her eyes were large and round and dark as polished buckeyes, deeply flecked with gold. Sprightly as a genie, endowed with a wealth of breeding and self-esteem, she viewed the world with an intensity of favor that piqued the wonder of strangers.

When she cleared her throat Carwood started nervously. Stefan looked lazily at his protégée, with the beginning of a wise smile. He sensed an intrigue.

Carwood said, "Perhaps you'd care to have a closer look, Miss Halloran? The light from the windows—"

"The light is fine." Echo settled back in her seat. She closed her eyes and touched the center of her forehead with two fingers. "I've seen enough. I'm very sorry, Mr. Carwood. But that canvas isn't David Herrera's work."

"Oh, my *dear*," Carwood said, drawing a pained breath as if he were trying to decide whether a tantrum or a seizure was called for, "you must be extremely careful about making potentially actionable judgments—"

"I am," Echo said, and opened her eyes wide, "always careful. It's a fake. And not the first fake Herrera I've seen. Give me a couple of hours and I'll tell you which of his students painted it, and when."

Carwood attempted to appeal to Stefan, who held up a cautionary finger.

"But that will cost you a thousand dollars for Miss Halloran's time and expertise. A thousand dollars an hour. I would advise you to pay it. She's very good. As for the lot you've shown us today—" Stefan got to his feet with a nod of good cheer. "Thank you for considering Gilbard's. I'm afraid our schedule is unusually crowded for the fall season. Why don't you try Sotheby's?"

For a man of his bulk, Stefan did a good job of imitating a capering circus bear in the elevator going down to the lobby of the Highbridge.

"Now, Stefan," Echo said serenely.

"But I *loved* seeing dear old Carwood go into the crapper."

"I didn't realize he was another of your old enemies."

"Enemy? I don't hold Charles in such high regard. He's simply a pompous ass. If he were mugged for his wits, he would only impoverish the thief. So tell me, who perpetrated the fraud?"

"Not sure. Either Fimmel or Arzate. Anyway, you can't get a fake Herrera past me."

"I'm sure it helps to have a photographic memory."

Echo grinned.

"Perhaps you should be doing my job."

"Now, Stefan." Echo reached out to press the second-floor button.

"Some day you *will* have my job. But you'll have to pry it from my cold, dead fingers."

Echo grinned again. The elevator stopped on two.

"What are you doing? Aren't we leaving?"

"In a little while." Echo stepped off the elevator and beckoned to Stefan. "This way."

"What? Where are you dragging me to? I'm desperate to have a smoke and find out how My Little Margie placed in the fourth."

Echo looked at her new watch, a twenty-second birthday present from her fiancé that she knew had cost far more than either of them should have been spending on presents.

"There's time. I want to see the Ransome they've borrowed for their show of twentieth-century portraitists."

"Oh, dear God!" But he got off the elevator with Echo. "I detest Ransome! Such transparent theatrics. I've seen better art on a sailor's ass."

"Really, Stefan?"

"Although not all that recently, I'm sorry to say."

The gallery in which the exhibition was being mounted was temporarily closed to the public, but they wore badges allowing them access to any part of the Highbridge. Echo ignored frowns from a couple of dithering functionaries and went straight to the portrait by Ransome that was already in place and lighted.

The subject was a seated nude, blond, Godiva hair. Ransome's style was impressionistic, his canvas flooded with light. The young woman was casually posed, like a Degas girl taking a backstage break, her face partly averted. Stefan had his usual attitude of near-suicidal disdain. But he found it hard to look away. Great artists were hypnotists with a brush.

"I suppose we must give him credit for his excellent eye for beauty."

"It's marvelous," Echo said softly.

"As Delacroix said, 'One never paints violently enough.' We must also give Ransome

credit for doing violence to his canvases.
And I must have an Armagnac, if the bar
downstairs is open. Echo?"

"I'm coming," she said, hands folded like
an acolyte's in front of her as she gazed up at
the painting with a faintly worshipful smile.

Stefan shrugged when she failed to budge.
"I don't wish to impose on your infatuation.
Suppose you join me in the limo in twenty
minutes?"

"Sure," Echo murmured.

Absorbed in her study of John Leland Ransome's technique, Echo didn't immediately
pay attention to that little barb at the back of
her neck that told her she was being closely
observed by someone.

When she turned she saw a woman standing twenty feet away ignoring the Ransome
on the wall, staring instead at Echo.

The woman was dressed all in black, which
seemed to Echo both obsessive and oppressive in high summer. But it was elegant, taste-
ful couture. She wasn't wearing jewelry. She
was, perhaps, excessively made up, but strik-

ing nonetheless. Mature, but Echo couldn't
guess her age. Her features were immobile,
masklike. The directness of her gaze, a burning in her eyes, gave Echo a couple of bad
moments. She knew a pickup line was coming. She'd averaged three of these encoun-
ters a week since puberty.

But the stare went on, and the woman said
nothing. It had the effect of getting Echo's
Irish up.

"Excuse me," Echo said. "Have we met?"
Her expression read, *Whatever you're thinking,
forget it, Queenie.*

Not so much as a startled blink. After a few
more seconds the woman looked rather deliberately from Echo to the Ransome painting on the wall. She studied that for a short
time, then turned and walked away as if Echo
no longer existed, heels clicking on the
gallery floor.

Echo's shoulders twitched in a spidery
spasm. She glanced at a portly museum
guard who also was eyeing the woman in
black.

"Who is *that?*"

The guard shrugged. "Beats me. She's

been around since noon. I think she's from the gallery in New York." He looked up at the Ransome portrait. "His gallery. You know how fussy these painters get about their placement in shows."

"Uh-huh. Doesn't she talk?"

"Not to me," the guard said.

The limousine Stefan had hired for the day was parked in a taxi zone outside the Highbridge. Stefan was leaning on the limo getting track updates on his BlackBerry. There was a *Daily Racing Form* lying on the trunk.

He put away his BlackBerry with a surly expression when Echo approached. My Little Margie must have finished out of the money.

"So the spell is finally broken. I suppose we could have arranged for a cot to be moved in for the night."

"Thanks for being so patient with me, Stefan."

They lingered on the sidewalk, enjoying balmy weather. New York had been a stewpot when they'd left that morning.

"It's all hype, you know," Stefan said, looking up at the gold and glass façade of the Cesar Pelli–designed building. "The Ransomes of the art world excel at manipulation. The scarcity of his work only makes it more desirable to the *vulturati*."

"No, I think it's the quality that's rare, Stefan. Courbet, Bonnard, he shares their sense of . . . call it a divine melancholy."

" 'Divine melancholy.' Nicely put. I must remember to filch that one for my *ARTnews* column. Where are we having dinner tonight? You *did* remember to make reservations? Echo?"

Echo was looking past him at the Woman in Black, who had walked out of the museum and was headed for a taxi.

Stefan turned. "Who, or what, is that?"

"I don't know. I saw her in the gallery. Caught her staring at me." Uncanny, Echo thought, how much she resembled the black queen on Echo's chessboard at home.

"Apparently, from her lack of interest now, you rebuffed her."

Echo shook her head. "No. Actually she never said a word. Dinner? Stefan, I'm sorry. You're set at Legal's with the Bronwyns for eight-thirty. But I have to get back to New

York. I thought I told you. Engagement party tonight. Peter's sister."

"Which sister? There seems to be a multitude."

"Siobhan. The last one to go."

"Not that huge, clumsy girl with the awful bangs?"

"Hush. She's really very sweet."

"Now that Peter has earned his gold shield, am I correct to assume the next engagement party will be yours?"

"Yes. As soon as we all recover from this one."

Stefan looked deeply aggrieved. "Echo, have you any idea what childbearing will do to your lovely complexion?"

Echo looked at her watch and smiled apologetically.

"I can just make the four o'clock Acela."

"Well, then. Get in."

Echo was preoccupied with answering e-mail during their short trip up Memorial Drive and across the river to Boston's South Station. She didn't notice that the taxi the Woman in Black had claimed was behind them all the way.

Hi Mom,
Busy day. I had to hustle but I made the four
o'clock train. I'll probably go straight to
Queens from the station so won't be home
until after midnight. Scored points with the
boss today; tell you all about it at breakfast.
Called Uncle Rory at the Home, but the
Sister on his floor told me he probably
wouldn't know who I was . . .

The Acela was rolling quietly through a tun-
nel on its way out of the city. In her coach seat
Echo, riding backwards, looked up from the
laptop she'd spent too much time with today.
Her vision was blurry, the back of her neck was
stiff, and she had a headache. She looked at
her reflection in the window, which disappeared as the train emerged into bright sunlight. She winced and closed her laptop after
sending the message to her mother, rum-
maged in her soft-leather shoulder bag for
Advil and swallowed three with sips of de-
signer water. Then she closed her eyes and
rubbed her temples.

When she looked up again she saw the
Woman in Black looking solemnly at her
before she opened the vestibule door and

disappeared in the direction of the club car.

The look didn't mean anything. The fact that they were on the same train didn't mean anything either. Even so for a good part of the trip to New York, while Echo tried to nap, she couldn't get the woman out of her mind.

Two

After getting eight stitches to close the cut near his left eye at the hospital in Flatbush, Peter O'Neill's partner Ray Scalla drove him to the 7-5 station house, where Pete retrieved his car and continued home to Bayside, Queens. By then he'd put in a twelve-hour day, but he had a couple of line-of-duty off days coming.

The engagement party for his sister Siobhan was roaring along by the time he got to the three-story brick-and-shingle house on Compton Place, and he had to hunt for a parking space a block and a half away. He walked back to the house swapping smack with neighborhood kids on their bikes and skateboards. The left eye felt swollen. He needed an ice bag, but a cold beer would be the first order of business. Make it two beers.

The O'Neill house was lit up to the roofline. Floodlights illuminated half a dozen guys playing a scuffling game of basketball in the driveway. Peter was related one way or another to all of them, and to everyone on the teeming porch.

His brother Tommy, a freshman at Hofstra on a football scholarship, fished in a tub of cracked ice and pitched Pete a twelve-ounce Rolling Rock as he walked up to the stoop. Kids with Game Boys cluttered the steps. His sister Kathleen, just turned thirty, was barefoot on the front lawn, gently rocking an infant to sleep on her shoulder. She gave Pete a kiss and frowned at the patched eye.

"So when's number four due?"

"You mean number five," Kathleen said. "October ninth, Petey."

"Guess I got behind on the count when I was workin' undercover." Pete popped the tab top on the icy Rock and drank half of it while he watched some of the half-court action on the driveway. He laughed. "Hey, Kath. Tell your old man to give up pasta or give up hoops."

Brother Tommy came down to the walk and put an arm around him. He was a linebacker, three inches taller than the five-eleven Peter but no wider in the shoulders. Big shoulders were a family hallmark, unfortunately for the women.

One of the basketball players got stuffed driving for a layup, and they both laughed.

"Hey, Vito!" Pete called. "Come on hard or keep it in your pants!" He finished off the beer and crushed the can. "Echo make it back from Boston?" he asked Tommy.

"She's inside. Nice shiner."

Pete said ruefully, "My collar give it to me."

"Too bad they don't hand out Purple Hearts downtown."

"Yeah, but they'll throw you a swell funeral," Pete said, forgetting momentarily what a remark like that meant to the women in a family of cops. Kathleen set him straight with a stinging slap to the back of his head. Then she crossed herself.

"God and Blessed Mother! Don't you ever say that again, Petey!"

Like the rest of the house, the kitchen was
full of people helping themselves to beer and
food. Peter gave his mom a kiss and looked at
Echo, who was taking a pan of hors d'oeuvres
out of the oven with oven mitts. She was moist
from the heat at her temples and under her
eyes. She gave Pete, or the butterfly patches
above his eye, a look and sat him down on a
stool near the door to the back porch for a
closer appraisal. Pete's middle sister Jessie
handed him a bulging hero.

"Little bitty girl," Pete said. "One of those
wiry types, you know? She was on crank and I
don't know what else."

"Just missed your eye," Echo said, tight-
lipped.

"Live and learn." Peter bit into his sandwich.

"You get a tetanus booster?"

"Sure. How was your day?"

"I did great," Echo said, still finding small
ways to fuss over him: brushing his hair back
from his forehead with the heel of one hand,
dabbing at a drip of sauce on his chin with a
napkin. "I deserve a raise."

"About time. How's your mom?"

"Didn't have a real good day, Julia said. Want another beer?"

"Makes you think I had one already?"

"Ha-ha," Echo said; she went out to the porch to fish the beer from the depths of the cooler. Peter's sister Siobhan, the bride-to-be, followed her unsteadily inside, back on her heels from an imaginary gale in her face. Her eyes not tracking well. She embraced Peter with a goofy smile.

"I'm so happy!"

"We're happy for you, Siobhan." At thirty-five she was the oldest of the seven O'Neill children, and the least well favored. Putting it mildly.

Her fiancé appeared in the doorway behind Siobhan. He was a head shorter, gap-toothed, had a bad haircut. A software salesman. Doing very well. He drove a Cadillac, had put a down payment on a condo in Valley Stream and was planning an expensive honeymoon cruise. The diamond on Siobhan's finger was a big one.

Peter saluted the fiancé with his can of beer. Siobhan straightened unsteadily and embraced Echo too, belching loudly.

"Oops. Get any on ya?"

"No, sweetie," Echo said, and passed her on to the fiancé, who chuckled and guided her through the kitchen to a bathroom. Peter shook his head.

"What they say about opposites."

"Yeah."

"Siobhan has a lot to learn. She still thinks 'fellatio' is an Italian opera."

"You mean it's not?" Echo said, wide-eyed. Then she patted his cheek. "Lay off. I love Siobhan. I love all your family."

Peter put the arm on his fourteen-year-old brother Casey as he came inside from the porch, and crushed him affectionately.

"Even the retards?"

"Get outta here," Casey said, fighting him off.

"Casey's no retard, he's a lover," Echo said. "Gimme a kiss, Case."

"No way!" But Echo had him grinning.

"Don't waste those on that little fart," Pete said.

Casey looked him over. "Man, you're gonna have a shiner."

"I know." Pete looked casually at Echo and put his sandwich down. "It's a sweatbox in here. Why don't we go upstairs a little while?"

Casey smiled wisely at them. "Uh-uh. Aunt Pegeen put the twins to sleep on your bed." He waited for the look of frustration in Peter's eyes before he said, "But I could let you use my room if you guys want to make out. Twenty bucks for an hour sound okay?"

"Sounds like you think I'm a hooker," Echo said to Casey. Staring him down. Casey's shoulders dropped; he looked away uneasily.

"I didn't mean—"

"Now you got a good reason not to skip confession again this week," Peter said. Glancing at Echo, and noticing how tired she looked, having lost her grip on her upbeat mood.

Driving Echo back to the city, Pete said, "I just keep goin' round and round with the numbers, like a dog chasin' its tail. You know?"

"Same here."

"Jesus, I'm twenty-six, ought to have my own place already instead of living home."

"*Our* own place. Trying to save anything

these days. The taxes. Both of us still paying off college loans. Forty thousand each. My mom sick. Your mom was sick—"

"We both got good jobs. The money'll come together. But we'll need another year."

Peter exited from the Queensboro Bridge and took First uptown. They were nearing 78th when Echo said, "A year. How bad can that be?" Her tone of voice said, *miserable.*

They waited on the light at 78th, looking at each other as if they were about to be cast into separate dungeons.

"Gotta tell you, Echo. I'm just goin' nuts. You know."

"I know."

"It hasn't been easy for you either. Couple close calls, huh?" He smiled ruefully.

She crossed her arms as if he'd issued a warning. "Yeah."

"You know what I'm sayin'. We are gonna be married. No doubt about that. Is there?"

"No."

"So—how big a deal is it, really? An act of contrition—"

"Pete, I'm not happy being probably the only twenty-two-year-old virgin on the face of the earth. But confession's not the same as getting a ticket fixed. You know how I was brought up. It's *God's law*. That has to mean something, or none of it does."

The light changed. Peter drove two blocks and parked by a fire hydrant a few doors down from Echo's brownstone.

"Both your parents were of the cloth," he said. "They renounced their vows and they made you. Made you for me. I can't believe God thought that was a sin."

Blue and unhappy, Echo sank lower in her seat, arms still crossed, over her breasts and her crucifix.

"I love you so much. And I swear to Him, I'll always take care of you."

After a long silence Echo said, "I know. What do you want me to do, Pete?"

"Has to be your call."

She sighed. "No motels. I feel cheap that way, I can't help myself. Just know it wouldn't work."

"There's this buddy of mine at the squad, he was in my year at the Academy, Frank Ringer. Like maybe you met him at the K of C picnic in July?"

"Oh. Yeah. Got a twitch in one eye? Really ripped, though."

"Right. Frank Ringer. Well, his uncle's got a place out on the Island. Way out, past Riverhead on Peconic Bay I think."

"Uh-huh."

"Frank's uncle travels a lot. Frank says he could make arrangements for us to go out there, maybe this weekend—"

"So you and Frank been having these discussions about our sex life?"

"Nothing like that. I just mentioned we'd both like to get off somewhere for some R and R, that's all."

"Uh-huh."

"So in exchange for the favor I'd cover Frank's security job for him sometime. Echo?"

"Guess I'd better be getting on up, see how mom is. Might be a long night; you know, I read to her when she can't—"

"So what do I tell Frank?"

Echo hesitated after she opened the door.

"This weekend sounds okay," she said. "Does his uncle have a boat?"

Three A.M. and John Leland Ransome, the painter, was up and prowling barefoot around his apartment at the Hotel Pierre on Fifth Avenue. The doors to his terrace were open; the sounds of the city's streets had dwindled to the occasional swish of cabs or a bus seven stories below. There was lightning in the west, a plume of yellow-tinged dark clouds over New Jersey or the Hudson. Some rain moving into Manhattan, stirring the air ahead of it. A light wind that felt good on his face.

Ransome had a woman on his mind. Not unusual; his life and career were dedicated to capturing the essence of a very few uniquely stunning creatures. But this was someone he'd never seen or heard of until approximately eight o'clock the night before. And the few photos he'd seen, taken with a phone cam, hadn't revealed nearly enough of Echo Halloran to register her so strongly on his imagination.

Anyway, it was too soon, he told himself. Better just to forget this one, the potential he'd glimpsed. His new show, the first in four years, was being mounted at his gallery. Five paintings only, his usual output after as much as eighteen painful months of work.

He wouldn't be ready to pick up a brush for at least that length of time. If ever again.

And half the world's population was women. More or less. A small but dependable percentage of them physically ravishing.

But this one was a painter herself, which intrigued him more than the one good shot of her he'd seen, taken on the train, Echo sitting back in her seat with her eyes closed, unaware that she was being photographed.

Ransome wondered if she had promise as a painter. But he could easily find out.

He lingered on the terrace until the first big drops of rain fell. He went inside, closing the doors, walked down a marble hall to the room in which Taja, wearing black silk lounging pajamas, was watching *Singin' in the Rain* on DVD. Another insomniac. She saw his reflection on the plasma screen and looked around. There was a hint of a contrite wince in his smile.

"I'll want more photos," he said. "Complete background check, of course. And order a car for tomorrow. I'd like to observe her myself."

Taja nodded, drew on a cigarette and returned her attention to the movie. Donald O'Connor falling over a sofa. She didn't smile. Taja never smiled at anything.

THREE

It rained all day Thursday; by six-thirty the clouds over Manhattan were parting for last glimpses of washed-out blue; canyon walls of geometric glass gave back the brassy sunset. Echo was able to walk the four blocks from her Life Studies class to the 14th Street subway without an umbrella. She was carrying her portfolio in addition to a shoulder tote and computer, having gone directly from her office at Gilbard's to class.

The uptown express platform was jammed, the atmosphere underground thick and fetid. Obviously there hadn't been a train for a while. There were unintelligible explanations or announcements on the P.A. Someone played a violin with heroic zeal. Echo edged her way up the platform to find breathing room where the first car would stop when the train got there.

Half a dozen Hispanic boys were scuffling,

cutting up; a couple of the older ones gave her the eye. One of them, whom she took in at a glance, looked like trouble. Tats and piercings. Full of himself.

A child of the urban jungle, Echo was skilled at minding her own business, building walls around herself when she was forced to linger in potentially bad company.

She pinned her bulky portfolio between her knees while she retrieved a half-full bottle of water from her tote. She was jostled from behind by a fat woman laden with shopping bags and almost lost her balance. The zipper on her portfolio had been broken for a while. A few drawings spilled out. Echo grimaced, nodded at the woman's brusque apology and tried to gather up her life studies before someone else stepped on them.

One of the younger Hispanic kids, wearing a do-rag and a Knicks jersey, came over to give her a hand. He picked up a charcoal sketch half-soaked in a puddle of water. Echo's problem had attracted the attention of all the boys.

The one she'd had misgivings about snatched the drawing from the hand of the Knicks fan and looked it over. A male nude.

He showed it around, grinning. Then backed off when Echo held out a hand, silently asking for the return of her drawing. She heard the uptown express coming.

The boy looked at her. He wore his *cholo* shirt unbuttoned to his navel.

"Who's this guy? Your boyfriend?"

"Give me a break, will you? I've had a long day, I'm tired, and I don't want to miss my train."

The boy pointed to the drawing and said, "Man, I seen a bigger tool on a gerbil."

They all laughed as they gathered around, reinforcing him.

"No," Echo said. "*My* boyfriend is on the cops, and I can arrange for you to meet him."

That provoked whistles, snorts, and jeers. Echo looked around at the slowing express train, and back at the boy who was hanging onto her drawing. Pretending to be an art critic.

"Hey, you're good, you know that?"

"Yes, I know."

"You want to do me, I can *arrange* the time." He grinned around at his buddies, one of whom said, "*Draw* you."

"Yeah, man. That's what I said." He

feigned confusion. "That ain't what I said?" He looked at Echo and shrugged magnanimously. "So first you draw me, then you can *do* me."

Echo said, "Listen, you fucking little idiot, I want my drawing *now*, or you'll be in shit up to your bull ring."

The express screeched to a stop behind her. A local was also approaching on the inside track. The boy made a show of being astonished by her threat. As if he were trembling in fright, his hands jerked and the drawing tore nearly in half.

"Oh, sorry, man. Now I guess you need to get yourself another naked guy." He finished ripping her drawing.

Echo, losing it, dropped her computer case and hooked a left at his jaw. She was quick on her feet; it just missed. The *cholo* danced away with the halves of the drawing in each hand, and bumped into a woman walking the yellow platform line of the local track as if she were a ballet dancer. The headlight of the train behind her winked on the slim blade of a knife in her right hand.

With her left hand she took hold of the

boy by his bunchy testicles and lifted him up on his toes until they were at eye level.

The Woman in Black stared at him, and the point of the knife was between two of his exposed ribs. Echo's throat dried up. She had no doubt the woman would cut him if he didn't behave. The boy's mouth was open, but he could have screamed without being heard as the train thundered by a couple of feet away from them.

The woman cast a long look at Echo, then nodded curtly toward the express.

The kid in the Knicks jersey picked up Echo's computer and shoved it at her as if he suspected that she too might have a blade. The doors of the local opened and there was a surge of humanity across the platform to the parked express. Echo let herself be carried along with it, looking back once as she boarded. Another glimpse of the Woman in Black, still holding the *cholo* helpless, getting a few looks but no interference. Echo's pulses throbbed. The woman was like a walking superstition, with a temperament as dark and lurking as paranoia.

Who was she? And why, Echo wondered as

the doors closed, does she keep showing up in *my* life?

She rode standing up to 86th in the jam of commuters, her face expressionless, presenting a calm front but inside just a blur, like a traumatized bird trying to escape through a sealed window.

Echo didn't say anything to Peter about the Woman in Black until Friday evening, when they were slogging along in oppressive traffic on the 495 eastbound, on their way to Mattituck and the cozy weekend they'd planned at the summer house of Frank Ringer's uncle.

"No idea who she is?" Peter said. "You're sure you don't know her from somewhere?"

"Listen, she's the kind, see her once, you never forget her. I'm talking spooky."

"She pulled a knife in the subway? Switchblade?"

"Maybe. I don't know much about knives. It was the look in her eyes, man. That *cholo* must've went in his pants." Echo smiled slightly, then her expression turned glum. "So, the first couple times, okay. Coincidence. A third time in the same week, uh-uh, I don't buy it. She must've been following me around." Echo shrugged again, and her shoulders stayed tight. "I didn't sleep so good last night, Pete."

"You ever see her again, make it your business to call me right away."

"I wonder if maybe I should—"

"*No.* Stay away from her. Don't try to talk to her."

"You're thinking she could be some sort of psycho?"

"That's New York. Ten people go by in the street, one or two out of the ten, something's gonna be seriously wrong with them mentally."

"Great. Now I'm scared."

Pete put an arm around her.

"You just let me handle this. Whatever it is."

"Engine's overheating." Echo observed.

"Yeah. Fucking traffic. Weekend, it'll be like this until ten o'clock. Might as well get off, get something to eat."

The cottage that had been lent to them for the weekend wasn't impressive in the headlights of Peter's car; it looked as if Frank Ringer's uncle had built it on weekends using materials taken from various construction or demolition sites. Mismatched windows, missing clapboards, a stone chimney on one side that obviously was out of plumb; the place had all the eye appeal of a bad scab.

"Probably charming inside," Echo said, determined to be upbeat about a slow start to their intimate weekend.

Inside the small rooms smelled of mildew from a leaky roof. There were curbsides in Manhattan that were better furnished on trash pickup days.

"Guess it's kind of like men only out here," Pete said, not concealing his disbelief. "I'll open a couple of windows."

"Do you think we could clean it up some?" Echo said.

Peter took another look around.

"More like burn it down and start over."

"It's such a beautiful little cove."

There was so much dismay in her face it started him laughing. He put an arm around her, guided her outside, and locked the door behind them.

"Live and learn," he said.

"Your house or mine?" Echo said.

"Bayside's closest."

The O'Neill house in Bayside didn't work out, either; overrun with relatives. At a few minutes past ten Echo unlocked the door of the Yorktown apartment where she lived with her mother and Aunt Julia, from her late father's side of the family. She looked at Peter, sighed, kissed him.

Rosemay and Julia were playing Scrabble at the dining room table when Echo walked in with Peter. She had left her weekend luggage in the hall by her bedroom door.

"This is a grand surprise," Rosemay said. "Echo, I thought you were stayin' over in Queens."

Echo cleared her throat and shrugged, letting Peter handle this one.

Pete said, "My uncle Dennis, from Philly? Blew into town with his six kids. Our house looks like a day camp. They been redoin' the walls with grape jelly." He bent over Rosemay, putting his arms around her. "How're you, Rosemay?"

Rosemay was wearing lounging pajamas and a green eyeshade. There were three support pillows in the chair she occupied, and one under her slippered feet.

"A little fatigued, I must say."

Julia was a roly-poly woman who wore thick eyeglasses. "Spent most of the day writing," she said of Rosemay. "Talk to your ma about eating, Echo."

"Eat, mom. You promised."

"I had my soft-boiled egg with some tea. It was, oh, about five o'clock, wasn't it, Julia?"

"Soft-boiled eggs. Wants nought but her bit of egg."

"They go down easy," Rosemay said, massaging her throat. Words didn't come easily, at least at this hour of the night. But for Rosemay sleep was elusive as well.

"All that cholesterol," Peter chided.

Rosemay smiled. "Nothing to worry about. I already have one fatal disease."

"None of that," Peter said sternly.

"Go on, Petey. You say what is. At least my mind will be the last of me to go. Pull up some chairs, we'll all play."

The doorbell rang. Echo went to answer it. Peter was arranging chairs around the table when he heard Echo unlock the door, then cry out.

"Peter!"

"Who is it, Echo?" Rosemay called, as Peter backtracked through the front room to the foyer. The door to the hall stood half open. Echo had backed away from the door and from the Woman in Black who was standing outside.

Peter took Echo by an elbow and flattened her against the wall behind the door, saying to the Woman in Black, "Excuse me, can I talk to you? I'm the police."

The Woman in Black looked at him for a couple of seconds, then reached into her purse as Peter filled the doorspace.

"Don't do that!"

The woman shook her head. She pulled something from her purse but Peter had a grip on her gloved wrist before her hand fully cleared. She raised her eyes to him but didn't resist. There was a white business card between her thumb and forefinger.

Still holding onto her wrist, Peter took the card from her with his left hand. Glanced at it. He felt Echo at his back, looking at the woman over his shoulder. The woman looked at Echo, looked back at Peter.

"What's going on?" Echo said, as Rosemay called again.

Peter let go of the Woman in Black, turned and handed Echo the card.

"Echo! Peter!"

"Everything's fine, mom," Echo said, studying the writing on the card in the dim foyer light.

Peter said to the Woman in Black, "Sorry I got a little rough. I heard about that knife you carry, is all."

This time it was Echo who moved Peter aside, opening the door wider.

"Peter, she can't—"

"Talk. I know." He didn't take his eyes off the woman in black. "You've got another card, tells me who you are?"

She nodded, glanced at her purse. Peter said, "Yeah, okay." This time the woman produced her calling card, which Echo took from her.

"Your name's Taja? Am I saying that right?"

The woman nodded formally.

"Taja what?"

She shrugged slightly, impatiently; as if it didn't matter.

"So I guess you know who *I* am. What did you want to see me about? Would you like to come in?"

"Echo—" Peter objected.

But the woman shook her head and indicated her purse again. She made an open-palm gesture, hand extended to Echo, slow enough so Peter wouldn't interpret it as hostile.

"You have something for me?" Echo said, baffled.

Another nod from Taja. She looked appraisingly at Peter, then returned to her purse and withdrew a cream-colored envelope the size of a wedding announcement.

Peter said, "Echo tells me you've been following her places. What's that about?"

Taja looked at the envelope in her hand as if it would answer all of their questions. Peter continued to size the woman up. She used cosmetics in almost theatrical quantities; that overload plus Botox, maybe, was enough to obscure any hint of age. She wore a flat-crowned hat and a long skirt with large fabric-covered buttons down one side. A scarlet puff of neckerchief was Taja's only concession to color. That, and the rose flush of her cheeks. Her eyes were almond-shaped, creaturely bold, intelligent. One thing about her, she didn't blink very often, which enhanced a certain robotic effect.

Echo took the envelope. Her name, hand-written, was on it. She smiled uncertainly at Taja, who simply looked away—something dismissive in her lack of expression, Peter thought.

"Just a minute. I'd like to ask you—"

The Woman in Black paused on her way to the stairs.

Echo said, "Pete? It's okay. Taja?"

Taja turned.

"I wanted to say—thank you. You know, for the subway, the other day?"

Taja, after a few moments, did something surprisingly out of character, considering her previous demeanor, the rigid formality. She responded to Echo with an emphatic thumbs-up before soundlessly disappearing down the stairs. Peter had the impression

she'd enjoyed intimidating the *cholo* kid.
Might have enjoyed herself even more if
she'd used the knife on him.

Echo had a hand on his arm, sensing his
desire to follow the Woman in Black.

"Let's see what this is," she said, of the envelope in her other hand.

"She looks Latin to me, what d'you think?"
Peter said to Echo as they returned to the
front room. Rosemay and Julia began talking at the same time, wanting to know who
was at the door. "Messenger," Peter said to
them, and looked out the windows facing
the street.

Echo, preoccupied, said, "You're the detective." She looked for a letter opener on
Rosemay's writing table.

"Jesus above," Julia said. "Sounded like a
ruckus. I was reachin' for me heart pills."

Peter saw the Woman in Black get into a
waiting limousine.

"Travels first class, whoever she is." He
caught the license plate number as the limo
pulled away, jotted it down on the inside of
his left wrist with a ballpoint pen.

Rosemay and Julia were watching Echo as
she slit the envelope open.

"What is it, dear, an invitation?"

"Looks like one."

"Now, who's getting married this time?" Julia said. "Seems like you've been to half a dozen weddings already this year."

"No, it's—" Echo's throat seemed to close up on her. She sat down slowly on one of a pair of matched love seats.

"Good news or bad?" Peter said, adjusting the blinds over the window.

"My . . . God!"

"Echo!" Rosemay said, mildly alarmed by her expression.

"This is so . . . utterly . . . fantastic!"

Peter crossed the room and took the invitation from her.

"But why me?" Echo said.

"Part of your job, isn't it? Going to these shows? What's so special about this one?"

"Because it's John Leland Ransome. And it's the event of the year. You're invited."

"I see that. 'Guest.' Real personal. I'm overwhelmed. Let's play." He took out his cell phone. "After I run a plate."

Echo wasn't paying attention to him. She had taken the invitation back and was staring at it as if she were afraid the ink might disappear.

Stefan Konine's reaction was predictable when Echo showed him the invitation. He pouted.

"Not to disparage your good fortune but, yes, why you? If I wasn't aware of your high moral standards—"

Echo said serenely, "Don't say it, Stefan."

Stefan began to look over a contract that one of his assistants had silently slipped onto his desk. He picked up his pen.

"I confess that it took me literally *weeks* to finagle my way onto the guest list. And I'm not just anyone's old hand job in this town."

"I thought you didn't like Ransome. Something about art on a sailor's—"

Stefan slashed through an entire paragraph on the contract and looked up at Echo.

"I don't worship the man, but I adore the event. Don't you have work to do?"

"I'm not strong on the pre-Raphaelites, but I called around. There's a definite lack of viability in today's market."

"Call it what it is, an Arctic chill. Tell the appraiser for the Chandler estate that he might do better on one of those auction-junkie internet sites." Stefan performed strong-arm surgery on another page of the contract. "You will want to appear in something singularly ravishing for the Ransome do. All of us at Gilbard's can only benefit from your reflected glory."

"May I put the gown on my expense account?"

"Of course not."

Echo winced slightly.

"But perhaps," Stefan said, twiddling his gold pen, "we can do something about that raise you've been whining about for weeks."

FOUR

Cyrus Mellichamp's personal quarters took up the fourth floor of his gallery on East 58th Street. They were an example of what wealth and unerring taste could accomplish. So was Cy himself. He not only looked pampered by the best tailors, dieticians, physical therapists, and cosmeticians, he looked as if he truly deserved it.

John Ransome's fortune was to the tenth power what Cy Mellichamp had managed to acquire as a kingpin of the New York art world, but on the night of the gala dedicated to himself and his new paintings, which he had no plans to attend, he was casually dressed. Tennis sweater, khakis, loafers. No socks. While the Mellichamp Gallery's guests were drinking Moët and Chandon below, Ransome sipped beer and watched the party on several TV monitors in Cy's study.

There was no sound, but thanks to the gallery owner's expensive surveillance system, it was possible, if he wanted, to tune in on nearly every conversation on the first two floors of the gallery, swarming with media-annointed superstars. Name a profession with glitter appeal, there was an icon, a living legend, or a luminary in attendance.

Cy Mellichamp had coaxed one of his very close friends, from a list that ran in the high hundreds, to prepare dinner for Ransome and his guests for the evening, both of whom were still unaware they'd been invited.

"John," Cy said, "Monsieur Rapaou wanted to know if there was a special dish you'd like added to his menu for the evening."

"Why don't we just scrap the menu and have cheeseburgers," Ransome said.

"Oh my God," Cy said, after a shocked intake of breath. "Scrap—? John, Monsieur Rapaou is one of the most honored chefs on four continents."

"Then he ought to be able to make a damn fine cheeseburger."

"Johnnn—"

"We're having dinner with a couple of kids. Basically. And I want them to be at ease, not worrying about what fork to use."

A dozen of the gallery's guests were being admitted at one time to the room in which the Ransome exhibition was mounted. To avoid damaged egos, the order in which they were being permitted to view the new Ransomes had been chosen impartially by lot. Except for Echo, Peter, and Stefan Konine, arbitrarily assigned to the second group. Ransome, for all of his indolence at his own party, was impatient to get on with his prime objective of the evening.

All of the new paintings featured the same model: a young black woman with nearly waist-length hair. She was, of course, smashing, with the beguiling quality that differentiates mere looks from classic beauty.

Two canvases, unframed, were wall-mounted. The other three, on easels, were only about three feet square. A hallmark of all Ransome's work were the wildly primeval, ominous or threatening landscapes in which his models existed aloofly.

Two minutes after they entered the room Peter began to fidget, glancing at Echo, who seemed lost in contemplation.

"I don't get it."

Echo said in a low firm tone, "Peter."

"What is it, like High Mass, I can't talk?"

"Just—keep it down, please."

"Five paintings?" Pete said, lowering his voice. "That's what all the glitz is about? The movie stars? Guy that plays James Bond is here, did you notice?"

"Ransome only does five paintings at a time. Every three years."

"Slow, huh?"

"Painstaking." Peter could hear her breathing, a sigh of rapture. "The way he uses light."

"You've been staring at that one for—"

"Go away."

Pete shrugged and joined Stefan, who was less absorbed.

"Does Ransome get paid by the square yard?"

"The square inch, more likely. It takes seven figures just to buy into the play-off round. And I'm told there are already more than four hundred prospective buyers, the cachet-stricken."

"For five paintings? Echo, just keep painting. Forget about your day job."

Echo gave him a dire look for breaking her concentration. Peter grimaced and said to Stefan, "I think I've seen this model somewhere else. *Sports Illustrated.* Last year's swimsuit issue."

"Doubtful," Stefan said. "No one knows who Ransome's models are. None of them have appeared at the shows, or been publicized. Nor has the genius himself. He might be in our midst tonight, but I wouldn't recognize him. I've never seen a photo."

"You saying he's shy?"

"Or exceptionally shrewd."

Peter had been focusing on a nude study of the unknown black girl. Nothing left to the imagination. Raw sensual appeal. He looked around the small gallery, as if his powers of detection might reveal the artist to him. Instead who he saw was Taja, standing in a doorway, looking at him.

"Echo?"

She looked around at Peter with a frown, then saw Taja herself. When the Woman in Black had her attention she beckoned. Echo and Peter looked at each other.

"Maybe it's another special delivery," Peter said.

"I guess we ought to find out."

In the center of the gallery's atrium a small elevator in a glass shaft rose to Cy Mellichamp's penthouse suite. A good many people who considered themselves important watched Peter and Echo rise to the fourth floor with Taja. Stefan took in some bemused and outright envious speculation.

A super-socialite complained, "I've spent seventeen million with Cy, and *I've* never been invited to the penthouse. Who *are* they?"

"Does Ransome have children?"

"Who knows?"

A talk-show host with a sneaky leer and a hard-drive's capacity for gossip said, "The dark one, my dear, is John Ransome's mistress. He abuses her terribly. So I've been told."

"Or perhaps it's the other way around," Stefan said, feeling a flutter of distress in his stomach that had nothing to do with the quantity of hors d'oeuvres he'd put away. Something was up, obviously it involved Echo, and even more obviously it was none of his business. Yet his impression, as he watched Echo step off the elevator and vanish into Cy's sanctum, was of a lovely doe being deftly separated from a herd of deer.

Taja ushered Echo and Peter into Cy Mellichamp's presence and closed the door to the lush sitting room, a gallery in itself that was devoted largely to French Impressionists. A very large room with a high tray ceiling. French doors opened onto a small terrace where there was a candlelit table set for three and two full-dress butlers in attendance.

"Miss Halloran, Mr. O'Neill! I'm Cyrus Mellichamp. Wonderful that you could be here tonight. I hope you're enjoying yourselves."

He offered his hand to Echo, and a discreet kiss to one cheek, somewhere between businesslike and avuncular, Peter noted. He shook hands with the man and they were eye to eye, Cy with a pleasant smile but no curiosity.

"We're honored, Mr. Mellichamp," Echo said.

"May I call you Echo?"

"Yes, of course."

"What do you think of the new Ransomes, Echo?"

"Well, I think they're—magnificent. I've always loved his work."

"He will be very pleased to hear that."

"Why?" Peter said.

They both looked at him. Peter had, deliberately, his cop face on. Echo didn't appreciate that.

"This is a big night for Mr. Ransome. Isn't it? I'm surprised he's not here."

Cy said smoothly, "But he is here, Peter."

Pete spread his hands and smiled inquiringly as Echo's expression soured.

"It's only that John has never cared to be the center of attention. He wants the focus to be solely on his work. But let John tell you himself. He's wanted very much to meet you both."

"Why?" Peter said.

"*Peter,*" Echo said grimly.

"Well, it's a fair question," Peter said, looking at Cy Mellichamp, who wore little gold tennis racket cuff links. A fair question, but not a lob. Straight down the alley, no time for footwork, spin on the return.

Cy blinked and his smile got bigger. "Of course it is. Would you mind coming with me? Just in the other room there, my study. Something we would like for you to see."

"You and Mr. Ransome," Peter said.

"Why, yes."

He offered Echo his arm. She gave Peter a swift dreadful look as she turned her back on him. Peter simmered for a couple of moments, took a breath and followed them.

The study was nearly dark. Peter was immediately interested in the array of security monitors, including three affording different angles on the small gallery where the newest Ransome paintings were on display. Where he had been with Echo a few minutes ago. The idea that they'd been watched from this room, maybe by Ransome himself, caused Peter to chew his lower lip. No reason Cy Mellichamp shouldn't have the best possible surveillance equipment to protect millions of dollars' worth of property. But so far none of this—Taja following Echo around town, the special invitations to Ransome's showing—added up, and Peter was more than ready to cut to the chase.

There was a draped, spotlighted easel to one side of Mellichamp's desk. The dealer walked Echo to it, smiling, and invited her to remove the drape.

"It's a work in progress, of course. John would be the first to say it doesn't do his subject justice."

Echo hesitated, then carefully uncovered the canvas, which revealed an incomplete study of—Echo Halloran.

Jesus, Peter thought, growing tense for no good reason. Even though what there was of her on the canvas looked great.

"Peter! Look at this!"

"I'm looking," Pete said, then turned, aware that someone had come into the room behind them.

"No, it doesn't do you justice," John Ransome said. "It's a beginning, that's all." He put out a hand to Peter. "Congratulations on your promotion to detective."

"Thanks," Pete said, testing Ransome's grip with no change of expression.

Ransome smiled slightly. "I understand your paternal grandfather was the third most-decorated officer in the history of the New York City police force."

"That's right."

Cy Mellichamp had blue-ribbon charm and social graces and the inward chilliness of a shark cruising behind the glass of an aquarium. John Ransome looked at Peter as if every detail of his face were important to recall at some later time. He held his grip longer than most men, but not too long. He was an inch taller than Peter, with a thick head of razor-cut hair silver over the ears, a square jawline softening with age, deep folds at the corners of a sensual mouth. He talked through his nose, yet the effect was sonorous, softly pleasing, as if his nose were lined with velvet. His dark eyes didn't veer from Peter's mildly contentious gaze. They were the eyes of a man who had fought battles, won only some of them. They wanted to tell you more than his heart could let go of. And that, Peter divined in a few moments of hand-to-hand contact with the man, was the major source of his appeal.

Having made Peter feel a little more at home Ransome turned his attention again to Echo.

"I had only some photographs," he said of the impressionistic portrait. "So much was missing. Until now. And now that I'm finally meeting you—I see how very much I've missed."

By candlelight and starlight they had cheeseburgers and fries on the terrace. And they *were* damn good cheeseburgers. So was the beer. Peter concentrated on the beer because he didn't like eating when something was eating him. Probably Echo's star-struck expression. As for John Leland Ransome—there was just something about aging yuppies (never mind the aura of the famous and reclusive artist) who didn't wear socks with their loafers that went against Peter's Irish grain.

Otherwise maybe it wasn't so hard to like

the guy. Until it became obvious that Ransome or someone else had done a thorough job of prying into Echo's life and family relations. Now hold on, just a damn minute.

"Your name is given as Mary Catherine on your birth and baptismal certificates. Where did 'Echo' come from?"

"Oh—well—I was talking a blue streak at eighteen months. Repeated everything I heard. My father would look at me and say, 'Is there a little echo in here?' "

"Your father was a Jesuit, I understand."

"Yes. That was his—vocation, until he met my mother."

"Who was teaching medieval history at Fordham?"

"Yes, she was."

"Now retired because of her illness. Is she still working on her biography of Bernard of Clairvaux? I'd like to read it sometime. I'm a student of history myself."

Peter allowed his beer glass to be filled for a fourth time. Echo gave him a vexed look as if to say, *Are you here or are you not here?*

Ransome said, "I see the beer is to your liking. It's from an exceptional little brewery in

Dortmund that's not widely known outside of Germany."

Peter said with an edge of hostility, "So you have it flown in by the keg, something like that?"

Ransome smiled. "Corner deli. Three bucks a pop."

Peter shifted in his seat. The lace collar of his tux was irritating his neck. "Mr. Ransome—mind if I ask you something?"

"If you'll call me John."

"Okay—John—what I'd like to know is, why all the detective work? I mean, you seem to know a h— a lot about Echo. Almost an invasion of her privacy, seems to me."

Echo looked as if she would gladly have kicked him, if her gown hadn't been so long. She smiled a tight apology to Ransome, but Peter had the feeling she was curious too, in spite of the hero worship.

Ransome took the accusation seriously, with a hint of contrition in his downcast eyes.

"I understand how that must appear to you. It's the nature of detective work, of course, to interpret my curiosity about Echo as suspicious or possibly predatory behavior.

But if Echo and I are going to spend a year together—"

"What?" Peter said, and Echo almost repeated him before pressing a napkin to her lips and clearing her throat.

Ransome nodded his point home with the confidence of those who are born and bred in the winner's circle; someone, Peter thought resentfully, who wouldn't break a sweat if his pants were on fire.

"—I find it helpful in my work as an artist," Ransome continued, "if there are other areas of compatibility with my subjects. I like good conversation. I've never had a subject who wasn't well read and articulate." He smiled graciously at Echo. "Although I'm afraid that I've tended to monopolize our table talk tonight." He shifted his eyes to Peter. "And Echo is also a painter of promise. I find that attractive as well."

Echo said incredulously, "Excuse me, I fell off at that last turn."

"Did you?" Ransome said.

But he kept his gaze on Peter, who had the look of a man being cunningly outplayed in a game without a rule book.

With the party over, the gallery emptied and cleanup crews at work, John Ransome conducted a personal tour of his latest work while Cy Mellichamp entertained Stefan Konine and a restless Peter, who had spent the better part of the last hour obviously wishing he were somewhere else. With Echo.

"Who is she?" Echo asked of Ransome's most recent model. "Or is that privileged information?"

"I'll trust your discretion. Her name is Silkie. Oddly enough, my previous subjects have remained anonymous at their own request. To keep the curious at arm's length. I suppose that during the year of our relationships each of them absorbed some of my own passion for—letting my work speak for itself."

"The year of your relationships? You don't see them any more?"

"No."

"Is that at your request?"

"I don't want it to seem to you as if I've had affairs that all turned out badly. That's far from the truth."

With her lack of expression Echo kept a guarded but subtle emotional distance from him.

"Silkie. The name describes her perfectly. Where is she from?"

"South Africa. Taja discovered her, on a train from Durban to Capetown."

"And Taja discovered me? She does get around."

"She's found all of my recent subjects—by 'recent' I mean the last twenty years." He smiled a bit painfully, reminded of how quickly the years passed, and how slowly he worked. "I very much depend on Taja's eye and her intuition. I depend on her loyalty. She was an artist herself, but she won't paint any more. In spite of my efforts to—inspire her."

"Why can't she speak?"

"Her tongue was cut out by agents of one of those starkly repressive Cold War governments. She wouldn't reveal the whereabouts of dissident members of her family. She was just thirteen at the time."

"Oh God, that's so awful!"

"I'm afraid it's the least of what was done to Taja. But she has always been like a—for want of a better word, *talisman* for me."

"Where did you meet her?"

"She was a sidewalk artist in Budapest, living down an alley with whores and thieves. I first saw her during one of my too-frequent sabbaticals in those times when I wasn't painting well. Nor painting very much at all. It's still difficult for me, nearly all of the time."

"Is that why you want me to pose for—a year?"

"I work for a year with my subject. Take another year to fully realize what we've begun together. Then—I suppose I just agonize for several months before finally packing my pictures off to Cy. And finally—comes the inevitable night."

He made a weary, sweeping gesture around the "Ransome Room," then brightened.

"I let them go. But this is the first occasion when I've had the good fortune of knowing my next subject and collaborator before my last paintings are out of our hands."

"I'm overwhelmed, really. That you would even consider me. I'm sorry that I have to say—it's out of the question. I can't do it."

Echo glanced past at him, to the doorway

where Peter was standing around with the other two men, trying not to appear anxious and irritable.

"He's a fine young man," Ransome said with a smile.

"It isn't just Peter, I mean, being away from him for so long. That would be hard. But there's my mother."

"I understand. I didn't expect to convince you at our first meeting. It's getting late, and I know you must be tired."

"Am I going to see you again?" Echo said.

"That's for you to decide. But I need you, Mary Catherine. I hope to have another chance to convince you of that."

Neither Echo nor Peter were the kind to be reticent about getting into it when there was an imagined slight or a disagreement to be settled. They were city kids who had grown up scrappy and contentious if the occasion called for it.

Before Echo had slipped out of the new shoes that had hurt her feet for most of the night she was in Peter's face. They were driving up Park. Too fast, in her opinion. She told him to slow down.

"Or put your flasher on. You just barely missed that cabbie."

"I can get suspended for that," Peter said.

"Why are you so *angry?*"

"Said I was angry?"

"It was a wonderful evening, and now you're spoiling it for me. *Slow down.*"

"When a guy comes on to you like that Ransome—"

"Oh, please. Comes *on* to me? That is so— so—I don't want to say it."

"Go ahead. We say what is, remember?"

"Im-mature."

"Thank you. I'm immature because the guy is stuffing me in the face and I'm supposed to—"

"Peter, I never said I was going to do it! I've got my job to think about. My mom."

"So why did he say he hoped he'd be hearing from you soon? And you just smiled like, *sure.* I can hardly wait."

"You don't just blow somebody off who has gone out of his way to—"

"Why not?"

"Peter. Look. I was paid an incredible compliment tonight, by a painter who I think is—I mean, I can't be flattered? Come on."

Peter decided against racing a red light and settled back behind the wheel.

"You come on. You got something arranged with him?"

"For the last time, *no.*" Her face was red, and she had chewed most of the gloss off her lower lip. In a softer tone she said, "You know it's not gonna happen, have some sense. The ball is over. Just let Cinderella enjoy her last moments, okay?—They're honking because the light is green, Petey."

Six blocks farther uptown Peter said, "Okay. I guess I—"

"Overreacted, what else is new? Sweetie, I love you."

"How much?"

"Infinity."

"Love you too. Oh God. Infinity."

Rosemay and Julia were asleep when Echo got home. She hung up the gown she'd worn to John Leland Ransome's show in her small closet, pulled on a sleep shirt and went to the bathroom to pee and brush her teeth. She spent an uncharacteristic amount of time studying her face in the mirror. It wasn't vanity; more as if she were doing an emotional self-portrait. She smiled wryly and shrugged and returned to her bedroom.

There she took down from a couple of shelves of cherished art books a slim oversized volume entitled *The Ransome Women*. She curled up against a bolster on her studio bed and turned on a reading lamp, spent an absorbed half hour looking over the thirty color plates and pages with areas of detail that illustrated aspects of the artist's technique.

She nodded off about three, then awoke with a start, the book sliding off her lap to the floor. Echo left it there, glanced at a landscape on her easel that she'd been working on for several weeks, wondering what John Ransome would think of it. Then she turned off the light and lay faceup in the dark, her rosary gripped unsaid in her fist. Thinking *what if, what if.*

But such a dramatic change in her life was solely in her imagination, or in a parallel universe. And *Cinderella* was a fairy tale.

FIVE

Peter O'Neill was working the day watch with his partner Ray Scalla, investigating a child-abuse complaint, when he was abruptly pulled off the job and told to report to the Commissioner's Office at One Police Plaza.

It was a breezy, unusually cool day in mid-September. Pete's lieutenant couldn't give him a reason for what was officially described as a "request."

"Downtown, huh?" Scalla said. "Lunch with your old man?"

"Jesus, don't ask me," Pete said, embarrassed and uncomfortable.

The offices of the Police Commissioner for the City of New York were on the fourteenth floor. Peter walked into reception to find his father also waiting there. Corin O'Neill was wearing his dress uniform, with the two stars of a borough commander. Pete would have been slightly less surprised to see Elvis Presley.

"What's going on, Pop?"

Corin O'Neill's smile was just a shade uneasy. "Beats me. Any problems on the job, Petey?"

"I'd've told you first."

"That you would."

The commissioner's executive assistant came out of her office. "Good morning, Peter. Glad you could make it."

As if he had a choice. Pete made an effort to look calm and slightly unimpressed. Corin said, "Well, Lucille. Let's find out how the wind's blowin' today."

"I just buzzed him. You can go right in, Commander."

But the commissioner opened his own door, greeting them heartily. His name was Frank Mullane.

"Well, Corin! Pleasure, as always. How is Kate? You know we've had a lot of concern."

"She's nearly a hundred percent now, and she'll be pleased you were askin'."

Mullane looked past him at Peter, then gave the young detective a partial embrace: handshake, bicep squeeze. "When's the last time I saw you, Peter? Rackin' threes for Cardinal Hayes?"

"I think so, yes, sir."

Mullane kept a hand on Peter's arm. "Come in, come in. So are you likin' the action in the 7–5?"

"That's what I wanted, sir."

As soon as they were inside the office, Lucille closing the door behind them, Peter saw John Ransome, wearing a suit and a tie today. It had been more than a month since the artist's show at the Mellichamp Gallery. Echo hadn't said another two words about Ransome; Peter had forgotten about him. Now he had a feeling that a brick was sinking to the pit of his stomach.

"Peter," Mullane said, "you already know John Ransome." Pete's father gave him a quick look. "John, this is Corin O'Neill, Pete's father, one of the finest men I've had on my watch."

The older men shook hands. Peter just stared at Ransome.

"John's an artist, I suppose you know," Mullane said to Corin. "My brother owns one of his paintings. And John has been a big supporter of police charities since well before I came to the office. Now, he has a little request, and we're happy to oblige him." Mullane turned and winked at Peter. "Special assignment for you. John will explain."

"I'm sure he will," Peter said.

A chartered helicopter flew Peter and John Ransome to the White Plains airport, where a limousine picked them up. They traveled north through Westchester County on Route 22 to Bedford. Estate country. They hadn't talked much on the helicopter, and on the drive through some of the most expensive real estate on the planet Ransome had phone calls to make. He was apologetic. Peter just nodded and looked out the window, feeling that his time was being wasted. He was sure that, eventually, Ransome was going to bring up Echo. He hadn't forgotten about her, and in his own quiet way he was a determined guy.

Once Ransome was off the phone for good Peter decided to go on the offensive.

"You live up this way?"

"I was raised here," Ransome said. "Bedford Village."

"So that's where we're going, your house?"

"No. The house I grew up in is no longer there. I let go of all but a few acres after my parents died."

"Must've been worth a bundle."

"I didn't need the money."

"You were rich already, is that it?"

"Yes."

"So—this special assignment the commissioner was talking about? You need for somebody to handle a, what, situation for you? Somebody causing you a problem?"

"You're my only problem at the moment, Peter."

"Okay, well, maybe I guessed that. So this is going to be about Echo?"

Ransome smiled disarmingly. "Do you think I'm a rich guy out to steal your girl, Peter?"

"I'm not worried. Echo's not gonna be your—what do you call it, your 'subject?' You know that already."

"I think there is more of a personal dilemma than you're willing to admit. It affects both you and Echo."

Peter shrugged, but the back of his neck was heating up.

"I don't have any personal dilemmas, Mr. Ransome. That's for guys who have too much time and too much money on their hands. You know? So they try to amuse themselves messin' around in other people's lives, who would just as soon be left alone."

"Believe me. I have no intention of causing either of you the slightest—" He leaned forward and pointed out the window.

"This may interest you. One of my former subjects lives here."

They were passing an estate enclosed by what seemed to be a quarter mile of low stone walls. Peter glimpsed a manor house in a grove of trees, and a name on a stone gatepost. Van Lier.

"I understand she's quite happy. But we haven't been in touch since Anne finished sitting for me. That was many years ago."

"Looks to be plenty well-off," Peter said.

"I bought this property for her."

Peter looked at him with a skeptical turn to his lips.

"All of my former subjects have been well provided for—on the condition that they remain anonymous."

"Why?"

"Call it a quirk," Ransome said, with a smile that mocked Peter's skepticism. "Us rich guys have all these quirks." He turned his attention to the road ahead. "There used to be a fruit and vegetable stand along this road that had truly wonderul pears and apples at this season. I wonder—yes, there it is."

Peter was thirsty and the cider at the stand was well chilled. He walked around while Ransome was choosing apples. Among the afternoon's shoppers was a severely disabled young woman in a wheelchair that looked as if it cost almost as much as a sports car.

When Ransome returned to the limo he asked Peter, "Do you like it up here?"

"Fresh air's giving me a headache. Something is." He finished his cider. "How many have there been, Mr. Ransome? Your 'subjects,' I mean."

"Echo will be the eighth. If I'm able to persuade—"

"No *if.* You're wasting your time." Peter looked at the helpless young woman in the wheelchair as she was being power-lifted into a van.

"ALS is a devastating disease, Peter. How long before Echo's mother can no longer care for herself?"

"She's probably got two or three years."

"And after that?"

"No telling. She could live to be eighty. If you want to call it living."

"A terrible burden for Echo to have to bear. Let's be frank."

Peter stared at him, crushing his cup.

"Financially, neither of you will be able to handle the demands of Rosemay's illness. Not and have any sort of life for yourselves. But I can remove that burden."

Peter put the crushed paper cup in a trash can from twenty feet away, turning his back on Ransome.

"Did you fuck all of them?"

"You know I have no intention of answering a question like that, Peter. I will say this: there can never be any conflict, any— hidden tension between my subjects and myself that will adversely affect my work. The work is all that really matters."

Peter looked around at him as blandly as he could manage, but the sun was in his eyes and they smarted.

"Here's what matters to us. Echo and me are going to be married. We know there're problems. We've got it covered. We don't need your help. Was there anything else?"

"I'm happy that we've had this time to become acquainted. Would you mind one more stop before we head back to the city?"

"Take your time. I'm on the clock, Pop said. So far it's easy money."

At the end of a winding uphill gravel drive bordered by stacked rock walls that obviously had been there for a century or longer, the limousine came to a pretty Cotswold-style stone cottage with slate roofs that overlooked a lake and a wildfowl sanctuary.

They parked on a cobblestone turnaround and got out. A caterer's van and a blue Land Rover stood near a separate garage.

"That's Connecticut a mile or so across the lake. In another month the view turns—well, as spectacular as a New England fall can be. In winter, of course, the lake is perfect for skating. Do you skate, Peter?"

"Street hockey," Peter said, taking a deep breath as he looked around. The sun was setting west of a small orchard behind the cottage; there was a good breeze across the hilltop. "So this is where you grew up?"

"No. The caretaker lived here. This cot-

tage and about ten acres of woods and orchard are all that's left of the five hundred
acres my family owned. All of it is now
deeded public land. No one can build another house within three-quarters of a mile."

"Got it all to yourself? Well, this is defi-
nitely where I'd work if I were you. Plenty of
peace and quiet."

"When I was much younger than you, just
beginning to paint, the woods in all their
form and color were like an appetite. Para-
phrasing Wordsworth, a different kind of
painter—poetry being the exotic pigment of
language." He looked slowly around, eyes
brimming with memory. "Almost six years
since I was up here. Now I spend most of my
time in Maine. But I recently had the cottage
redecorated, and added an infinity pool on
the lake side. Do you like it, Peter?"

"I'm impressed."

"Why don't you have a look around inside?"

"Looks like you've got company. Anyway,
what's the point?"

"The point is, the cottage is yours, Peter. A
wedding present for you and Echo."

Peter had hit a trifecta two years ago at

Aqueduct, which rewarded him with twenty-six hundred dollars. He'd been thrilled by the windfall. Now he was stunned. When his heartbeat was more or less under control he managed to say, "Wait a minute. You . . . can't do this."

"It's done, Peter. Echo is in the garden, I believe. Why don't you join her? I'll be along in a few minutes."

"Omigod, Peter, do you *believe* it?"

She was on the walk that separated garden and swimming pool, the breeze tugging her hair across her eyes. There were a lot of roses in the garden, he noticed. He felt, in spite of the joy he saw in Echo's face, a thorn in his heart. And it was a crushing effort for him just to breathe.

"Jesus, Echo—what've you done?"

"Peter—"

He walked through the garden toward her. Echo sat on a teakwood bench, hands folded in her lap, her pleasure dimmed to a defensive smile because she knew what was coming. He could almost see her stubborn streak surfacing, like a shark's fin in blood-ied waters. Peter made an effort to keep his tone reasonable.

"Wedding present? That's china and toast-ers and things. How do we rate something like this? Nobody in his right mind would give away—"

"I haven't done anything," Echo said. "And it isn't ours. Not yet."

"I'm usually in my right mind," John Ran-some said pleasantly. Peter stopped, halfway between Echo and Ransome, who was in the doorway to the garden, the setting sun mak-ing of his face a study in sanguinity. He held a large thick envelope in one hand. "Escrow to the cottage and grounds will close in one year, when Mary Catherine has completed her obligation to me." He smiled. "I don't ex-pect an invitation to the wedding. But I wish you both a lifetime of happiness. I'll leave this inside for you to read." Nobody said any-thing for a few moments. They heard a heli-copter. Ransome glanced up. "My ride is here," he said. "Make yourselves at home for as long as you like, and enjoy the dinner I've had prepared for you. My driver will take you back to the city when you're ready to go."

The night turned unseasonably chilly for mid-September, temperature dropping into the low fifties by nine o'clock. One of the caterers built a fire on the hearth in the garden room while Echo and Peter were served after-dinner brandies. They sipped and read the contract John Ransome had left for Echo to sign, Peter passing pages to her as he finished reading.

A caterer looked in on them to say, "We'll be leaving in a few minutes, when we've finished cleaning up the kitchen."

"Thank you," Echo said. Peter didn't look up or say a word until he'd read the last page of the contract. Wind rattled one of the stained-glass casement windows in the garden room. Peter poured more brandy for himself, half a snifter's worth, as if it were cherry Coke. He drank all of it, got up and paced while Echo read by firelight, pushing her reading glasses up the bridge of her nose with a forefinger when they slipped.

When she had put the twelve pages in order, Peter fell back into the upholstered chair opposite Echo. They looked at each other. The fire crackled and sparked.

"I can't go up there to see you? You can't come home, unless it's an emergency? He doesn't want to paint you, he wants to own you!"

They heard the caterer's van drive away. The limo chauffeur had enjoyed his meal in a small apartment above the garage.

"I understand his reasons," Echo said. "He doesn't want me to be distracted."

"Is that what I am? A distraction?"

"Peter, you don't have a creative mind, so I really don't expect you to get it." Echo frowned; she knew when she sounded condescending. "It's only for a year. I can *do* this. Then we're set." She looked around the garden room, a possessive light in her eyes. "My Lord, this place, I've never even dreamed of— I want Mom to see it! Then, if she approves—"

"What about my approval?" Peter said with a glower, drinking again.

Echo got up and stretched. She shuddered. In spite of the fire it was a little chilly in the room. He watched the rise and fall of her breasts with blurred yearning.

"I want that too."

"And you want this house."

"Are you going to sulk the rest of the evening?"

"Who's sulking?"

She took the glass from his hand, sat down in his lap and cradled her head on a wide shoulder, closing her eyes.

"With real estate in the sky, best we could hope for is a small house in, you know, Yonkers or Port Chester. This is *Bedford.*"

Peter cupped the back of her head with his hand.

"He's got you wanting, instead of thinking. He's damn good at it. And that's how he gets what *he* wants."

Echo slipped a hand over his heart. "So angry." She trembled. "I'm cold, Peter. Warm me up."

"Isn't what we've always planned good enough any more?"

"Oh, Peter. I love you and I'm going to marry you, and nothing will ever change that."

"Maybe we should get started home."

"But what if this *is* home, Peter? Our home." She slid off his lap, tugged nonchalantly at him with one hand. "C'mon. You haven't seen everything yet."

"What did I miss?" he said reluctantly.

"Bedroom. And there's a fireplace too."

She dealt soothingly with his resistance, his fears that he wasn't equal to the emotional cost that remained to be exacted for their prize. He wasn't steady on his feet. The brandy he had drunk was hitting him hard.

"Just think about it," Echo said, leading him. "How it could be. Imagine that a year has gone by—so fast—," Echo kissed him and opened the bedroom door. Inside there was a gas log fire on a corner hearth. "And here we are." She framed his his face lovingly with her hands. "What do you want to do now?" she said, looking solemnly into his eyes.

Peter swallowed the words he couldn't speak, glancing at the four-poster bed that dominated the room.

"I know what I want you to do," she said.

"Echo—"

She tugged him into the room and closed the door with her foot.

"It's all right," she said as he wavered. "Such a perfect place to spend our first night together. I want you to appreciate just how much I love you."

She left him and went to a corner of the

room by the hearth where she undressed quickly, a quick-change artist, down to the skin, slipping then beneath covers, to his fuming eyes a comely shadow.

"Peter?"

He touched his belt buckle, dropped his hands. He felt at the point of tears; ardor and longing were compromised by too much drink. His heartbeat was fueled by inchoate anger.

"Peter? What's wrong?"

He took a step toward her, stumbled, fell against a chair with a lyre back. Heavy, but he lifted it easily and slammed it against the wall. His unexpected rage had her cowering, his insulted hubris a raw wound she was too inexperienced to deal with. She hugged herself in shock and pain.

Peter opened the bedroom door.

"I'll wait in the fuckin' limo. You—you stay here if you want! Stay all night. Do whatever the hell you think you've got to do to make yourself happy, and just never mind what it'll do to us!"

SIX

The first day of fall, and it was a good day for riding in convertibles: unclouded blue sky, temperatures on the East Coast in the sixties. The car John Ransome drove uptown and parked opposite Echo's building was a Mercedes two-seater. Not a lot of room for luggage, but she'd packed frugally, only the clothes she would need for wintering on a small island off the coast of Maine. And her paintbox.

He didn't get out of the car right away; cell phone call. Echo lingered an extra few moments at her bedroom windows hoping to see Peter's car. They'd talked briefly at about one A.M., and he'd sounded okay, almost casual about her upcoming forced absence from his life. Holidays included. He was trying a little too hard not to show a lack of faith in her. Neither of them mentioned John Ransome. As if he didn't exist, and she was leaving to study painting in Paris for a year.

Echo picked up her duffels from the bed and carried them out to the front hall. She left the door ajar and went into the front room where Julia was reading to Rosemay from the *National Enquirer*. Julia was a devotee of celebrity gossip.

Commenting on an actress who had been photographed trying to slip out of a California clinic after a makeover, Julia said, "Sure and she's at an age where she needs to give up plastic surgery and place her bets with a good taxidermist."

Rosemay smiled, her eyes on her daughter. Rosemay's lips trembled perceptibly; her skin was china-white, mimicking the tone of the bones within. Echo felt a strong pulse of fear; how frail her mother had become in just three months.

"Mom, I'm leaving my cell phone with you. It doesn't work on the island, John says. But there's a dish for Internet, no problem with e-mail."

"That's a blessing."

"Peter comin' to see you off?" Julia asked.

Echo glanced at her watch. "He wasn't sure. They were working a triple homicide last night."

"Do we have time for tea?" Rosemay asked, turning slowly away from her computer and looking up at Echo through her green eyeshade.

"John's here already, mom."

Then Echo, to her surprise and chagrin, just lost it, letting loose a flood of tears, sinking to her knees beside her mother, laying her head in Rosemay's lap as she had when she was a child. Rosemay stroked her with an unsteady hand, smiling.

Behind them John Ransome appeared in the hallway. Rosemay saw his reflection on a window pane. She turned her head slowly to acknowledge him. Julia, oblivious, was turning the pages of her gossip weekly.

The expression in Rosemay's eyes was more of a challenge than a welcome to Ransome. Her hands came together protectively over Echo. Then she prayerfully bowed her head.

Peter double-parked in the street and was running up the stairs of Echo's building when he met Julia coming down with her Save the Trees shopping bag.

"They're a half hour gone, Peter. I was just on my way to do the marketing."

Peter shook his head angrily. "I only got off a half hour ago! Why couldn't she wait for me, what was the big rush?"

"Would you mind sittin' with Rosemay while I'm out? Because it's goin' down hard for her, Peter."

He found Rosemay in the kitchen, a mug of cold tea between her hands. He put the kettle on again, fetched a mug for himself and sat down wearily with Rosemay. He took one of her hands in his.

"A year. A year until she's home again. Peter, I only let her do this because I was afraid—"

"It's okay. I'll be comin' around myself, two, three times a week, see how you are."

"—not afraid for myself," Rosemay said, finishing her thought. "Afraid of what my illness could do to you and Echo."

They looked at each other wordlessly until the kettle on the stove began whistling.

"Listen, we're gonna get through this," Peter said, grim around the mouth.

Rosemay's head drooped slowly, as if she hadn't the strength to hold it up any longer.

"He came, and took her away. Like the old days of lordship, you see. A privilege of those who ruled."

———

Echo didn't see much of Kincairn Island that night when they arrived. The seven-mile ferry trip left her so sick and sore from heaving she couldn't fully straighten up once they docked at the fishermen's quay. There were few lights in the clutter of a town occupying a small cove. A steady wind stung her ears on the short ride cross island by Land Rover to the house facing two thousand miles of open ocean.

A sleeping pill knocked her out for eight hours.

At first light the cry of gulls and waves booming on the rocks a hundred feet below her bedroom windows woke her up. She had a hot shower in the recently updated bathroom. Some eyedrops got the red out. By then she thought she could handle a cup of black coffee. Outside her room she found a flight of stairs to the first-floor rear of the house. Kitchen noises below. John Ransome was an early riser; she heard him talking to someone.

The kitchen also had gone through a recent renovation. But the architect hadn't disturbed quaint and mostly charming old features: a hearth for baking in one corner, hand-hewn oak beams overhead.

"Good morning," John Ransome said. "Looks as if you got your color back."

"I think I owe you an apology," Echo mumbled.

"For getting sick on the ferry? Everybody does until they get used to it. The fumes from that old diesel banger are partly to blame. How about breakfast? Ciera just baked a batch of her cinnamon scones."

"Coffeecoffeecoffee," Echo pleaded.

Ciera was a woman in her sixties, olive-skinned, with tragic dark eyes. She brought the coffeepot to the table.

"Good morning," Echo said to her. "I'm Echo."

The woman cocked her head as if she hadn't heard correctly.

"It's just a—a nickname. I was baptized Mary Catherine."

"I like Mary Catherine," Ransome said. He was smiling. "So why don't we call you by your baptismal name while you're here."

"Okay," Echo said, with a glance at him. It wasn't a big thing; nicknames were childish

anyway. But she felt a slight psychic disturbance. As if, in banishing "Echo," he had begun to invent the person whom he really
wanted to paint, and to live within a relationship that he firmly controlled.

Foolish, Echo thought. *I know who I am.*

The rocky path to the Kincairn lighthouse,
where Ransome had his studio, took them
three hundred yards through scruffy stunted
hemlock and blueberry barrens, across
lichen-gilded rock, thin earth, and frost-
heaves. At intervals the path wended close to
the high-tide line. Too close for Echo's
peace of mind, although she tried not to appear nervous. Kincairn Island, about eight
and a half crooked miles by three miles wide
with a high, forested spine, was only a
granitic pebble confronting a mighty ocean,
blue on this October morning beneath a
lightly cobwebbed sky.

"The light is fantastic," she said to Ransome.

"That's why I'm here, in preference to
Cascais or Corfu for instance. Clear winter
mornings are the best. The town is on the
lee side of the island facing Penobscot.

There's a Catholic church, by the way, that the diocese will probably close soon, or Unitarian for those who prefer Religion Lite."

"Who else lives here?" Echo asked, blinking salt spume from her eyelashes. The tide was in, wind from the southeast.

"About a hundred forty permanent residents, average age fifty-five. The economy is lobsters. Period. At the turn of the century Kincairn was a lively summer community, but most of the old saltbox cottages are gone; the rest belong to locals."

"And you own the island?"

"The original deed was recorded in 1794. You doing okay, Mary Catherine?"

The ledge they were crossing was only about fifty feet above the breakers and a snaggle of rocks close to shore.

"I get a little nervous . . . this close."

"Don't you swim?"

"Only in pools. The ocean—I nearly drowned on a beach in New Jersey. I was five. The waves that morning were nothing, a couple of feet high. I had my back to the water, playing with my pail and shovel. All of a sudden there was a huge wave, out of nowhere, that caught everybody by surprise."

"Rogue wave. We get them too. My parents were sailing off the light, just beyond that nav buoy out there, when a big one capsized their boat. They never had a chance."

"Good Lord. When was this?"

"Twenty-eight years ago." The path took a turn uphill, and the lighthouse loomed in front of them. "I'm a strong swimmer. Very cold water doesn't seem to get to me as quickly as other people. When I was nineteen—and heavily under the influence of Lord Byron—I swam the Hellespont. So I've often wondered—" He paused and looked out to sea. "If I had been with my mother and father that day, could I have saved them?"

"You must miss them very much."

"No. I don't."

After a few moments he looked around at her, as if her gaze had made him uncomfortable.

"Is that a terrible thing to say?"

"I guess I— I don't understand it. Did you love your parents?"

"No. Is that unusual?"

"I don't think so. Were they abusive?"

"Physically? No. They just left me alone most of the time, as if I didn't exist. I don't know if there's a name for that kind of pain."

His smile, a little dreary, suggested that they leave the topic alone. They walked on to the lighthouse, brilliantly white on the highest point of the headland. Ransome had remodeled it, to considerable outrage from purists, he'd said, installing a modern, airport-style beacon atop what was now his studio.

"I saw what it cost you," Ransome said, "to leave your mother—your life. I'd like to think that it wasn't only for the money."

"Least of all. I'm a painter. I came to learn from you."

He nodded, gratified, and touched her shoulder.

"Well. Shall we have a look at where we'll both be working, Mary Catherine?"

Peter didn't waste a lot of time taking on a load at the reception following his sister Siobhan's wedding to the software salesman from Valley Stream. Too much drinking gave him the mopes, followed by a tendency to take almost anything said to him the wrong way.

"What've you heard from Echo?" a first cousin named Fitz said to him.

Peter looked at Fitz and had another swallow of his Irish in lieu of making conversation. Fitz glanced at Peter's cousin Rob Flaherty, who said, "Six tickets to the Rangers tonight, Petey. Good seats."

Fitz said, "That's two for Rob and his girl, two for me and Colleen, and I was thinkin'— you remember Mary Mahan, don't you?"

Peter said ungraciously, "I don't feel like goin' to the Rangers, and you don't need to be fixin' me up, Fitz." His bow tie was hanging limp and there was fire on his forehead and cheekbones. A drop of sweat fell unnoticed from his chin into his glass. He raised the glass again.

Rob Flaherty said with a grin, "You remind me of a lovesick camel, Petey. What you're needin' is a mercy hump."

Peter grimaced hostilely. "What I need is another drink."

"Mary's had a thing for you, how long?"

"She's my mom's godchild, asshole."

Fitz let the belligerence slide. "Well, you know. It don't exactly count as a mortal sin."

"Leave it, Fitz."

"Sure. Okay. But that is exceptional pussy you're givin' your back to. I can testify."

Rob said impatiently, "Ah, let him sit here and get squashed. Echo must've tied a knot in his dick before she left town with her artist friend."

Peter was out of his chair with a cocked fist before Fitz could step between them. Rob had reach on Peter and jabbed him just hard enough in the mouth to send him backwards, falling against another of the tables ringing the dance floor, scarcely disturbing a mute couple like goggle-eyed blowfish, drunk on senescence. Pete's mom saw the altercation taking shape and left her partner on the dance floor. She took Peter gently by an elbow, smiled at the other boys, telling them with a motion of her elegantly coiffed head to move along. She dumped ice out of a glass onto a napkin.

"Dance with your old ma, Peter."

Somewhat shamefaced, he allowed himself to be led to the dance floor, holding ice knotted in the napkin to his lower lip.

"It's twice already this month I see you too much in drink."

"It's a wedding, Ma." He put the napkin in a pocket of his tux jacket.

"I'm thinking it's time you get a grip on yourself," Kate said as they danced to a slow beat. "You don't hear from Echo?"

"Sure. Every day."

"Well, then? She's doing okay?"

"She says she is." Peter drew a couple of troubled breaths. "But it's e-mail. Not like actually—you know, hearin' her voice. People are all the time sayin' what they can't put into words, you just have to have an ear for it."

"So—maybe there's things she wants you to know, but can't talk about?"

"I don't know. We've never been apart more than a couple days since we met. Maybe Echo's found out—it wasn't such a great bargain after all." He had a tight grip on his mother's hand.

"Easy now. If you trust Echo, then you'll hold on. Any man can do that, Petey, for the woman he loves."

"I'll always love her," Peter said, his voice

tight. He looked into Kate's eyes, a fine simmer of emotion in his own eyes. "But I don't trust a man nobody knows much about. He's got walls around him you wouldn't believe."

"A man who values his privacy. That kind of money, it's not surprising." Kate hesitated. "You been digging for something? Unofficially, I mean."

"Yeah."

"No beefs?"

"No beefs. The man's practically invisible where public records are concerned."

"Then let it alone."

"If I could see Echo, just for a little while. I'm half nuts all the time."

"God love you, Peter. Long as you have Sunday off, why don't the two of us go to visit Rosemay, take her for an outing? Been a while since I last saw her."

"I don't think I can, Ma. I, uh—need to go up to Westchester, talk to somebody."

"Police business, is it?"

Peter shook his head.

"Her name's Van Lier. She posed for John Ransome once."

SEVEN

The Van Lier residence was a copy—an exact copy, according to a Web site devoted to descriptions of Westchester County's most spectacular homes—of a sixteenth-century English manor house. All Peter saw of the inside was a glimpse of slate floor and dark wainscotting through a partly opened front door.

He said to the houseman who had answered his ring, "I'd like to see Mrs. Van Lier."

The houseman was an elderly Negro with age spots on his caramel-colored face like the spots on a leopard.

"There's no *Mrs.* Van Lier at this residence."

Peter handed him his card.

"Anne Van Lier. I'm with the New York police department."

The houseman looked him over patiently, perhaps hoping if his appraisal took long enough Peter would simply vanish from their doorstep and he could go back to his nap.

"What is your business about, Detective? Miss Anne don't hardly care to see nobody."

"I'd like to ask her a few questions."

They played the waiting game until the

houseman reluctantly took a Motorola Talk-
about from a pocket of the apron he wore
over his Sunday suit and tried to raise her on
a couple of different channels. He frowned.

"Reckon she's laid hers down and forgot
about it," he said. "Well, likely you'll find
Miss Anne in the greenhouse this time of the
day. But I don't expect she'll talk to you, police or no police."

"Where's the greenhouse?"

"Go 'round the back and walk toward the
pond, you can't hardly miss it. When you see
her, tell Miss Anne I did my best to raise her
first, so she don't throw a fit my way."

Peter approached the greenhouse through
a squall of copper beech leaves on a windy afternoon. The slant roofs of the long greenhouse reflected scudding clouds. Inside a
woman he assumed was Anne Van Lier was
visible through a mist from some overhead
pipes. She wore gloves that covered half of
her forearms and a gardening hat with a
floppy brim that, along with the mist floating
above troughs of exotic plants, obscured
most of her face. She was working at a potting
bench in the diffused glimmer of sunlight.

"Miss Van Lier?"

She stiffened at the sound of an unfamiliar voice but didn't look around. She was slight-boned in dowdy tan coveralls.

"Yes? Who is it?" Her tone said that she didn't care to know. "You're trespassing."

"My name is Peter O'Neill. New York City police department."

Peter walked a few steps down a gravel path toward her. With a quick motion of her head she took him in and said, "Stay where you are. Police?"

"I'd like to show you some identification."

"What is this about?"

He held up his shield. "John Leland Ransome."

She dropped a three-pronged tool from her right hand onto the bench and leaned against it as if suddenly at a loss for breath. Her back was to Peter. A dry scuttle of leaves on the overhead glass cast a kaleidoscope of shadow in the greenhouse. He wiped mist from his forehead and continued toward her.

"You posed for Ransome."

"What of it? Who told you that?"

"He did."

She'd been rigidly still; now Anne Van Lier seemed pleasurably agitated.

"You *know* John? You've seen him?"

"Yes."

"When?"

"A couple of months ago." Peter had closed the distance between them. Anne darted another look his way, a gloved hand covering her profile as if she were a bashful child; but she no longer appeared to be concerned about him.

"How is John?" Her voice was suddenly rich with emotion. "Did he—mention me?"

"That he did," Peter said reassuringly, and dared to ask, "Are you still in love with Ransome?"

She shuddered, protecting herself with the glove as if he'd thrown a stone, seeming to cower.

"What did John say about me? *Please.*"

Knowing he'd touched a nerve, Peter said soothingly, "Told me the year he spent with you was one of the happiest of his life."

Still it bothered him when, after a few moments, she began softly to weep. He moved closer to Anne, put a hand on her arm.

"Don't," she pleaded. "Just go."

"How long since you seen him last, Anne?"

"Eighteen years," she said despondently.

"He also said—it was his understanding that you were very happy."

Anne Van Lier gasped. Then she began shaking with laughter, as if at the cruelest joke she'd ever heard. She turned suddenly to Peter, knocking his hand away from her, snatching off her gardening hat as she stared up at him.

The shock she gave him was like the electric jolt from a hard jab to the solar plexus. Because her once-lovely face was a horror.

She had been brutally, deeply slashed. Attempts had been made to correct the damage, but plastic surgeons could do only so much. Repairing damage to severed nerves was beyond any surgeon's skill. Her mouth drooped on one side. She had lost the sight of her left eye, filled now with a bloom of suffering.

"Who did this to you? Was it Ransome?"

Jarred by the blurted question, she backed away from Peter.

"What? *John?* How dare you think that!"

Gloved fingers prowled the deep disfiguring lines on her face.

"I never saw my attacker. It happened on a

street in the East Village. He could have been a mugger. I didn't resist him, so why, *why?*"

"The police—"

"Never found him." She stared at Peter, and through him, at the past. "Or is that what you've come to tell me?"

"No. I don't know anything about the case. I'm sorry."

"Oh. Well." Her fate was dead weight on her mind. "So many years ago."

She put her gardening hat back on, adjusted the brim, gave Peter a vague look. She was in the past again.

"You can tell John—I won't always look like this. Just one more operation, they promised. I've had ten so far. Then I'll—finally be ready for John." She anticipated the question Peter wasn't about to ask. "To pose again!" A vaguely flirtatious smile came and went. "Otherwise I've kept myself up, you know. I do my exercises. Tell John—I bless him for his patience, but it won't be much longer."

In spite of the humidity and the drifting spray in the greenhouse Peter's throat was dry. His own attempt at a smile felt like hardening plaster on his face. He knew he had only glimpsed the depths of her psychosis. The decent thing to do now was to leave her with some assurance that her fantasy would be fulfilled.

"I'll tell him, Miss Van Lier. That's the news he's been waiting for."

The following Saturday night Peter was playing pool with his old man at the Knights of Columbus, and letting Corin win. The way he used to let him win at Horse when Corin was still spry enough for some basketball: *Just a little off my game tonight*, Pete would always say, pretending annoyance. Corin bought the beers afterward and they relaxed in a booth at their favorite sports bar.

"Heard you was into the cold case files in the Ninth," Corin said, wiping some foam off his mustache. He looked at one of the big screens around the room. The Knicks were at the Heat, and tonight they couldn't throw one in the ocean.

"You hear everything, Pop," Pete said admiringly.

"In my borough. What's up?"

"Just something I got interested in, I had a

little spare time." He explained about the Van Lier slashing.

"How many times was she cut?"

"Ten slashes, all on her face. He just kept cutting on her, even after she was down. That sound like all he wanted was a purse?"

"No. Leaves three possibilities. A psycho, hated women. Or an old boyfriend she gave the heave-ho to, his ego couldn't take it. But you said the vic didn't make him."

"No."

"Then somebody hired it done. Tell me again what your interest is in the vic?"

"Eighteen, nineteen years ago, she posed for John Ransome."

Corin rubbed a temple and managed to keep his disapproval muted. "Jeez Marie, Petey."

"My girl is up there in Maine with him, Pop!"

"And you're lettin' your imagination—I see your mind workin'. But it's far-fetched, lad. Far-fetched."

"I suppose so," Peter mumbled in his beer.

"How many young women do you think have posed for him in his career?"

"Seven that anybody knows about. Not counting Echo."

Corin spread his hands.

"But nobody knows who they are, or where they are. Almost nobody, it's some kind of secret list. I'm tellin' you, Pop, there is too much about him that don't add up."

"That's not cop sense, that's your emotions talkin'."

"Two damn months almost, I don't see her."

"That was his deal. His and hers, and there's good reasons why Echo did it."

"Didn't tell you this before. That woman friend of his, whore, whatever: she carries a knife and Echo saw her almost use it on a kid in the subway."

"Jeez Marie, where's this goin' to end with you?" Corin sat back in the booth and rapped the table once with the knuckles of his right fist. "Tell you where it ends. Right here, tonight. You know why? Too much money, Petey. That's what it's always about."

"Yeah, I know. I saw the commissioner's head up Ransome's ass."

"Remember that." He stared at Peter until exasperation softened into forgiveness. "Echo have any problems up there she's told you about?"

"No," Peter admitted. "Ransome's just do-

ing a lot of sketches of her, and she has time
to paint. I guess everything's okay."

"Give her credit for good sense, then. And
do your part."

"Yeah, I know. Wait." His expression was
pure naked longing and remorse. "Two
months. And you know what, Pop? It's like
one of us died. Only I don't know which
one, yet."

As she had done almost every day since arriv-
ing on Kincairn Echo took her breakfast in
chilly isolation in a corner of the big kitchen,
then walked to the lighthouse. Frequently
she could see only a few feet along the path
because of fog. But sometimes there was no
fog; the air was sharp and windless as the rising sun cast upon the copper face of the sea
a great peal of morning.

She'd learned early on that John Ransome
was an insomniac who spent most of the
deep night hours reading in his second-floor
study or taking long walks by himself in the
dark, with only a flashlight along island paths
he'd been familiar with since he was a boy.

Sleep would come easier for him, Ransome assured her, as if apologizing, once he settled down to doing serious painting. But the unfinished portrait he'd begun in New York on a big rectangle of die board had remained untouched on his easel for nearly six weeks while he devoted himself to making postcard-size sketches of Echo, hundreds of them, or silently observing her own work take shape. Late at night he would leave Post-it Notes of praise or criticism on her easel.

When they were together he was always cordial but preferred letting Echo carry the conversation. He seemed endlessly curious about her life. About her father, who had been a Jesuit until the age of fifty-one, when he met Rosemay, a Maryknoll nun. He never asked about Peter.

There were days when Echo didn't see him at all. She felt his absence from the island but had no idea of where he'd gone, or why. Not that it was any of her business. But it wasn't the working relationship she'd bargained for. His inability to resume painting made her uneasy. And it wasn't her nature to put up with being ignored, or feeling slighted, for long.

"Is it me?" she'd asked him at dinner the night before.

Her question, the mood of it, startled him.

"No. Of course not, Mary Catherine." He looked distressed, random gestures substituting for the words he couldn't find to reassure her. "Case of nerves, that's all. It always happens. I'm afraid I'll begin and—then I'll find myself drawing from a dry well." He paused to pour himself more wine. He'd been drinking more before and after dinner than was his custom; his aim was a little off and he grimaced. "Afraid that everything I do will be trite and awful."

Echo had sensed his vulnerability—all artists had it. But she wasn't quite sure how to deal with his confession.

"You're a great painter."

Ransome shook his head, shying from the burden of her suggestion.

"If I ever believe that, then I will be finished." Echo got up, pinched some salt from a silver bowl, and spread it over the wine stain on the fine linen tablecloth. She looked hesitantly at him.

"How can I help?"

He was looking at the salted stain. "Does that work?"

"Usually, if you do it right away."

"If human stains were so easy to remove," he said with sudden vehemence.

"God's always listening," she said, then thought it was probably too glib, patronizing, and unsatisfactory. She felt God, but she also felt there was little point in trying to explain Him to someone else.

After a silence the unexpected flood of his passion ebbed.

"I don't believe as easily as you, Mary Catherine," he said with a tired smile that became tense. "But if we do have your God watching us, then I think it likely that his revenge is to do nothing."

Ransome pushed his chair back and stood, looked at Echo, put out a hand and lifted her head slightly with thumb and forefinger on her chin. He said, studying her as if for the first time, "The light in your eyes is the light from your heart."

"That's sweet," Echo said demurely, knowing what was coming next. She'd been thinking about it, and how to handle it, for weeks.

He kissed her on the forehead, not the lips, as if bestowing a blessing. That was sweet too. But the erotic content, enough to cause her lips to part and put a charge in her heartbeat, took her by surprise.

"I have to leave the island for a few days," he said then.

Ransome's studio had replaced the closetlike space that once had held the Kincairn light and reflecting mirror. It sat upon the spindle of the lighthouse shaft like a flying saucer made mostly of glass that was thirty feet in diameter. There was an elevator inside, another addition, but Echo always used the circular stairs coming and going. Ciera was a very good cook and the daily climb helped Echo shed the pounds that had a tendency to creep aboard like hitchhikers on her hips.

She had decided, because the day was neither blustery enough to blow her off her Vespa nor bitterly cold, to pack up her paints and easel and go cross island for an exercise in plein air painting on the cove and dock.

Approaching Kincairn village, Echo saw John Ransome at the end of the town dock unmooring a cabin cruiser that had been tied up alongside Wilkins' Marine and the mail/ferry boat slip. She stopped her puttering scooter in front of the cottage where a lone priest, elderly and in virtual exile in this most humble of parishes, lived with an equally old housekeeper. Echo had no reason for automatically keeping her distance from Ransome until she also saw Taja at the helm of the cruiser, which wasn't much of a reason either. She hadn't seen the Woman in Black nor given her much thought since the night of the artist's show at Cy Mellichamp's. Ransome never mentioned her. Apparently she seldom visited the island.

Friend, business associate, confidante? Mistress, of course. But if she kept some distance between them now, perhaps that was in the past. Even if they were no longer lovers Echo assumed she might still be emotionally supportive, a rare welcome visitor to his *isolato* existence—his stiller doom, Echo thought with a certain poignancy, remembering a phrase of Charlotte Bronte's from Echo's favorite novel, *Jane Eyre*.

Watching Ransome jump into the bow of the cruiser, Echo felt frustrated for his sake. Obviously he was not going to be painting anytime soon. She also felt a dim sense of betrayal that made no sense to her. Yet it lingered like the spectral imprint of a kiss that had made her restless during a night of confused, otherworldly dreams; dreams of Ransome, dreams of being as naked in his studio as a snail on a thorn.

Echo watched Taja back the cruiser from the dock and turn it toward the mainland, pour on the power. She decided to take a minute to go into the empty church. Was it time to ring the bell for a confession of her own? She couldn't make up her mind about that, and her heart was no help either.

Cy Mellichamp was using a phone at a gallery associate's desk in the second-floor office when Peter was brought in by a secretary. Mellichamp glanced at him with no hint of welcome. Two more associates, Mellichamp's morale-boosting term for salespeople, were working the phones and computers. In another large room behind the office paintings were being uncrated.

Mellichamp smiled grievously at something he was hearing and fidgeted until he had a chance to break in.

"Really, Allen, I think your affections are misplaced. There is neither accomplishment nor cachet in the accident of Roukema's success. And at six million—no, I don't want to have this conversation. *No.* The man should be doing frescoes in tombs. You wanted my opinion, which I freely give to you. Okay, please think it over and come to your senses."

Cy rang off and looked again at Peter, with the fixed smile of a man who wants you to understand he could be doing better things with his time.

"Why," he asked Peter, "do otherwise bright young people treat inherited fortunes the way rednecks treat junk cars?" He shrugged. "Mr. O'Neill! Delighted to see you again. How can I help you?"

"Have you heard anything from Mr. Ransome lately?"

"We had dinner two nights ago at the Four Seasons."

"Oh, he was in town?" Cy waited for a more sensible question. "His new paintings sell okay?"

"We did very, very well. And how is Echo?"

"I don't know. I'm not allowed to see her, I might be a distraction. I thought Ransome was supposed to be slaving away at his art up there in Maine."

Cy looked at his watch, looked at Peter again uncomprehendingly.

"I was hoping you could give me some information, Mr. Mellichamp."

"In regard to?"

"The other women Ransome has painted. I know where one of them lives. Anne Van Lier." The casual admission was calculated to provoke a reaction; Peter didn't miss the slight tightening of Cy Mellichamp's baby blue eyes. "Do you know how I can get in touch with the others?"

Cy said after a few moments, "Why should you want to?" with a muted suggestion in his gaze that Peter was up to no good.

"Do you know who and where those women are?"

An associate said to Cy, "Princess Steph on three."

Distracted, Cy looked over his shoulder. "Find out if she's on St. Barts. I'll get right back to her."

While Cy wasn't watching him Peter glanced at a computer on a nearby desk where nobody was working. But the person whose desk it was had carelessly left his user ID on the screen.

Cy looked around at Peter again. "I could not help you if I did know," he said curtly. "Their whereabouts are none of my business."

"Why is Ransome so secretive about those women?"

"That, of course, is John's prerogative. Now if you wouldn't mind—it *has* been one of those days—" He summoned a moment of the old charm. "I'm sorry."

"Thanks for taking the time to see me, Mr. Mellichamp."

"If there should be a next time, unless it happens to be official, you would do well to leave that gold shield in your pocket."

EIGHT

Peter got home from his watch at twenty past midnight. He fixed himself a sardine sandwich on sourdough with a smelly slice of gouda and some salsa dip he found in the fridge. He carried the sandwich and a bottle of Sam Adams up the creaky back stairs to the third floor he shared with his brother Casey. The rest of the house was quiet except for his father's distant whistling snore. But with no school for two days Case was still up with his iMac. Graphics were Casey's passion: his ambition was to design the cars of the future.

Peter changed into sweats. The third floor was drafty; a wind laced with the first fitful snow of the season was belting them.

There was an e-mail on the screen of his laptop that said only *missyoumissyoumissyou.* He smiled bleakly, took a couple of twenties from his wallet and walked through the bathroom he shared with Casey, pausing to kick a wadded towel off the floor in the direction of the hamper.

"Hi, Case."

Casey, mildly annoyed at the intrusion, didn't look around.

"That looks like the Batmobile," Peter said of the sleek racing machine Casey was refining with the help of some Mac software.

"It is the Batmobile."

Peter laid a twenty on the desk where Casey would see it out of the corner of his eye.

"What's that for?"

"For helping me out."

"Doing what?"

"See, I've got this user ID, but there's probably gonna be a log-on code too—"

"Hack a system?"

"I'm not stealing anything. Just want to look at some names, addresses."

"It's against the law."

Peter laid the second twenty on top of the first.

"Way I see it, it's kind of a gray area. There's something going on, maybe involves Echo, I need to know about. Right away."

Casey folded the twenties with his left hand and slid them under his mouse pad.

"If I get in any trouble," he said, "I'm givin' your ass up first."

After nearly a week of Ransome's absence, Echo was angry at him, fed up with being virtually alone on an island that every storm or squall in the Atlantic seemed to make a pass at almost on a daily basis, and once again dealing with acute bouts of homesickness. Never mind that her bank account was automatically fattening twice a month, it seemed to be payment for emotional servitude, not the pleasant collaboration she'd anticipated. Only chatty e-mails from girlfriends, from Rosemay and Stefan and even Kate O'Neill, plus Peter's maddeningly noncommittal daily communications (he was hopeless at putting feelings into words), provided balance and escape from depression through the long nights. They reminded her that the center of her world was a long way from Kincairn Island.

She had almost no one to talk to other than the village priest, who seemed hard put to remember her name at each encounter, and Ransome's housekeeper. But Ciera's idea of a lively conversation was two sentences an hour. Much of the time, perhaps affected by the dismal weather that smote their rock or merely the oppression of passing time, Ciera's face looked as if Death had scrawled an "overdue" notice on it.

Echo had books and her music and DVDs of recent movies arrived regularly. She had no difficulty in passing the time when she wasn't working. But she hated the way she'd been painting lately, and missed the stealth insights from her employer and mentor. Day after day she labored at what she came to judge as stale, uninspired landscapes, taking a palette knife to them as soon as the light began to fade. She didn't know if it was the creeping ennui or a faltering sense of confidence in her talent.

November brought fewer hours of the crystal lambency she'd discovered on her first day there. Ransome's studio was equipped with full-spectrum artificial light, but she always preferred painting outdoors when it was calm enough, no tricky winds to snatch her easel and fling it out to sea.

The house of John Ransome, built to outlast centuries, was not a house in which she would ever feel at home, in spite of his library and collection of paintings that included some of his own youthful work that would never be shown anywhere. These she studied with the avid eye of an archaeologist in a newly unearthed pyramid. The house was stone and stout enough but at night in a hard gale had its creepy, shadowy ways. Hurricane lamps had to be lit two or three times a week at about the same time her laptop lost satellite contact and the screen's void reflected her dwindled good cheer. Reading by lamplight hurt her eyes. Even with earplugs she couldn't fall asleep when the wind was keening a single drawn-out note or slapdash, grabbing at shutters, mewling under the eaves like a ghost in a well.

Nothing to do then but lie abed after her rosary and cry a little as her mood worsened. And hope John Ransome would return soon. His continuing absence a puzzle, an irritant; yet working sorcery on her heart. When she was able to fall asleep it was Ransome whom she dreamed about obsessively. While fitful and half awake she recalled every detail of a self portrait and the faces of his women. Had any of his subjects felt as she now did? Echo wondered about the depth of each relationship he'd had with his unknown beauties. One man, seven young women—had Ransome slept with any of them? Of course he had. But perhaps not every one.

His secret. Theirs. And what might other women to come, lying awake in this same room on a night as fierce as this one, adrift in loneliness and sensation of their own, imagine about Echo's involvement with John Leland Ransome?

Echo threw aside her down comforter and sat on the edge of the bed, nervous, heart-heavy. Except for hiking shoes she slept fully dressed, with a small flame in one of the tarnished lamp chimneys for company and a hammer on the floor for security, not knowing who in that island community might take a notion, no matter what the penalty. Ciera went home at night to be with her severely arthritic husband, and Echo was alone.

She rubbed down the lurid gooseflesh on her arms, feeling guilty in the sight of God for what raged in her mind, for sexual cravings like nettles in the blood. She put her hand on the Bible beside her bed but didn't open it. *Dear Lord, I'm only human.* She felt, honestly, that it was neither the lure of his flesh nor the power of his talent but the mystery of his torment that ineluctably drew her to Ransome.

A shutter she had tried to secure earlier was loose again to the incessant prying of the wind, admitting an almost continual flare of lightning centered in this storm. She picked up the hammer and a small eyebolt she'd found in a tool chest along with a coil of picture wire.

It was necessary to crank open one of the narrow lights of the mullioned window, getting a faceful of wind and spume in the process. As she reached for the shutter that had been flung open she saw by a run of lightning beneath boiling clouds a figure standing a little apart from the house on the boulders that formed a sea wall. A drenched white shirt ballooned in the wind around his torso. He faced the sea and the brawling waves that rose ponderously to foaming heights only a few feet below where he precariously stood, waves that crashed down with what seemed enough force to swamp islands larger than Kincairn.

John Ransome had returned. Echo's lips parted to call to him, small-voiced in the tumult. Her skin crawled coldly from fear, but the shutter slammed shut on her momentary view of the artist.

When she pushed it open again and leaned out slightly to see him, her eyelashes matting with salt spray, hair whipping around her face, Ransome had vanished.

Echo cranked the window shut and backed away, tingling in her hands, at the back of her neck. She took a few deep breaths, wiping at her eyes, then turned, grabbed a flashlight and went to the head of the stairs down the hall from her room, calling his name in the darkness, shining the beam of the light down the stairs, across the foyer to the front door, which was closed. There was no trace of water on the floor, as she would have expected if he'd come in out of the storm.

"ANSWER ME, JOHN! ARE YOU HERE?"

Silence, except for the wind.

She bolted down the stairs, grabbed a hooded slicker off the wall-mounted coat tree in the foyer and let herself out.

The three-cell flashlight could throw a brilliant beam for well over a hundred yards. She looked around with the light, shuddering in the cold, lashed in a gale that had to be more than fifty knots. She heard thunder rolling above the shriek of the wind. She was scared to the marrow. Because she knew she had to leave the relative shelter afforded by the house at her back and face the sea where she'd last seen him.

With her head low and an arm protecting her face, she made her way to the seawall, the dash of waves terrifying in the beam of the flashlight. Her teeth were clenched so tight she was afraid of chipping them. Remembering the shock of being engulfed on what had been a calm day at the Jersey shore, pulled tumbling backwards and almost drowning in the sandy undertow.

But she kept going, mounted the seawall and crouched there, looking down at the monster waves. It was near to freezing. In spite of the hood and slicker she was already soaked and trembling so badly she was afraid of losing her grip on the flashlight as she crawled over boulders. Looking down into crevices where he might have fallen, to slowly drown at each long roll of a massive wave.

Thought she saw something—something alive like an animal caught in discarded plastic wrap. Then she realized it was a face she was looking at in the down-slant of the flashlight, and it wasn't plastic, it was Ransome's white shirt. He lay sprawled on his back a few feet below her, dazed but not unconscious. His eyelids squinched in the light cast on his face.

Echo got down from the boulder she was on, found some footing, got her hands under his arms and tugged.

One of his legs was awkwardly wedged between boulders. She couldn't tell if it was broken as she turned her efforts to pulling his foot free. Hurrying. Her strength ebbing fast. Battling him and the storm and sensing something behind her, still out to sea but coming her way with such size, unequaled in its dark momentum, that it would drown them both in one enormous downfall like a building toppling.

"MOVE!"

Echo had him free at last and pushed him frantically toward the top of the seawall. She'd managed to lose her grip on the flashlight but it didn't matter, there was lightning around their heads and all of the deep weight of the sea coming straight at them. She couldn't make herself look back.

Whatever the condition of his leg, Ransome was able to hobble with her help. They staggered toward the house, whipsawed by the wind, until the rogue wave she'd anticipated burst over the seawall and sent them rolling helplessly a good fifty feet before its force was spent.

When she saw Ransome's face again beneath the flaring sky he was blue around the mouth but his eyes had opened. He tried to speak but his chattering teeth chopped off the words.

"WHAT?"

He managed to say what was on his mind between shudders and gasps.

"I'm n-n-not w-worth it, y-you know."

Hot showers, dry clothing. Soup and coffee when they met again in the kitchen. When she had Ransome seated on a stool she looked into his eyes for sign of a concussion, then examined the cut on his forehead, which was two inches long and deep enough so that it would probably scar. She pulled the edges of the cut together with butterfly bandages. He sipped his coffee with steady hands on the mug and regarded her with enough alertness so that she wasn't worried about that possible concussion.

"How did you learn to do this?" he asked, touching one of the bandages.

"I was a rough-and-tumble kid. My parents weren't always around, so I had to patch myself up."

He put an inquisitive fingertip on a small scar under her chin.

"Street hockey," she said. "And this one—"

Echo pulled her bulky fisherman's sweater high enough to reveal a larger scar on her lower rib cage.

"Stickball. I fell over a fire hydrant."

"Fortunately . . . nothing happened to your marvelous face."

"Thanks be to God." Echo repacked the first aid kit and ladled clam chowder into large bowls, straddled a stool next to him. "Ought to see my knees," she said, as an afterthought. She was ravenous, but before dipping the spoon into her chowder she said, "You need to eat."

"Maybe in a little while." He uncorked a bottle of brandy and poured an ounce into his coffee.

Echo bowed her head and prayed silently, crossed herself. She dug in. "And thanks be to God for saving our lives out there."

"I didn't see anyone else on those rocks. Only you."

Echo reached for a box of oyster crackers. "Do I make you uncomfortable?"

"How do you mean, Mary Catherine?"

"When I talk about God."

"I find that . . . endearing."

"But you don't believe in Him. Or do you?"

Ransome massaged a sore shoulder.

"I believe in two gods. The god who creates and the god who destroys."

He leaned forward on the stool, folded his arms on the island counter, which was topped with butcher block, rested his head on his arms. Eyes still open, looking at her as he smiled faintly.

"The last few days I've been keeping company with the god who destroys. You have a good appetite, Mary Catherine."

"Haven't been eating much. I don't like eating alone at night."

"I apologize for—being away for so long."

Echo glanced thoughtfully at him.

"Will you be all right now?"

He sat up, slipped off his stool, stood behind her and put a hand lightly on the back of her neck.

"I think the question is—after your experience tonight, will *you* be all right—with me?"

"John, were you trying to kill yourself?"

"I don't think so. But I don't remember what I was thinking out there. I'm also not sure how I happened to find myself sitting naked on the floor of the shower in my bathroom, scrubbed pink as a boiled lobster."

Echo put her spoon down. "Look, I cut off your clothes with scissors and sort of bullied you into the shower and loofah'd you to get your blood going. Nothing personal. Something I thought I'd better do, or else. I left clothes out for you then went upstairs and took a shower myself."

"You must have been as near freezing as I was. But you helped me first. You're a tough kid, all right."

"You were outside longer than me. How much longer I didn't know. But I knew hypothermia could kill you in a matter of minutes. You had all of the symptoms."

Echo resumed eating, changing hands with the spoon because she felt as if her right hand was about to cramp; it had been doing that for an hour.

She had cut off his clothes because she wanted him naked. Not out of prurience; she'd been scared and angry and needed to distance herself from his near-death folly and the hard reality of the impulse that had driven him outside in his shirt and bare feet to freeze or drown amid the rocks. Nude, barely conscious, and semicoherent, the significance of *Ransome* was reduced in her mind and imagination; sitting on the floor of the shower and shuddering as the hot water drove into him, he was to her like an anonymous subject in a life class, to be viewed objectively without unreliable emotional investment. It gave her time to think about the situation. And decide. If it was only creative impotence there was still a chance she could be of use to him. Otherwise she might as well be aboard when the ferry left at sunrise.

"Mary Catherine?"

"Yes?"

"I've never loved a woman. Not one. Not ever. But I may be in love with you."

She thought that was too pat to take seriously. A compliment he felt he owed her. Not that she minded the mild pressure of his palm on her neck. It was soothing, and she had a headache.

Echo looked around at Ramsome. "You're bipolar, aren't you?"

He wasn't surprised by her diagnosis.

"That's the medical term. Probably all artists have a form of it. Soaring in the clouds or morbid in the depths, too blue and self-pitying to take a deep breath."

Echo let him hold her with his gaze. His fingers moved slowly along her jawline to her chin. She felt that, all right. Maybe it was going to become an issue. He had the knack of not blinking very often that could be mesmerizing in a certain context. She lifted her chin away from his hand.

"My father was manic-depressive," she said. "I learned to deal with it."

"I know that he didn't kill himself."

"Nope. Chain-smoking did the job for him."

"You were twelve?"

"Just twelve. He died on the same day that I got—my—when I—"

She felt that she had blundered—*Way too personal, Echo*—and shut up.

"Became a woman. One of the most beautiful women I've been privileged to know. I feel that in a small way I may do your father honor by preserving that beauty for—who knows? Generations to come."

"Thank you," Echo said, still resonant

from his touch, her brain on lull. Then she got what he was saying. She looked at Ransome again in astonishment and joy. He nodded.

"I feel it beginning to happen," he said. "I need to sleep for a few hours. Then I want to go back to that portrait of you I began in New York. I have several ideas." He smiled rather shyly. "About time, don't you think?"

NINE

After a few days of indecision, followed by an unwelcome intrusion that locked two seemingly unrelated incidents together in his mind, Cy Mellichamp made a phone call, then dropped around to the penthouse apartment John Ransome maintained at the Hotel Pierre. It was snowing in Manhattan. Thanksgiving had passed, and jingle bell season dominated Cy's social calendar. Business was brisk at the gallery.

The Woman in Black opened the door to Cy, admitting him to the large gloomy foyer, where she left him standing, still wearing his alpaca overcoat, muffler, and Cossack's hat.

Cy swallowed his dislike for and mistrust of Taja and pretended he wasn't being slighted by John Ransome's gypsy whore. And who knew what else she was to Ransome in what had the appearance, to Mellichamp, of a folie à deux relationship.

"We were hacked last night," he said. "Whoever it was now has the complete list of Ransome women. Including addresses, of course."

Taja cocked her head slightly, waiting, the low light of a nearby sconce repeated in her dark irises.

"The other, ah, visitation might not be germane, but I can't be sure. Peter O'Neill came to the gallery a few days ago. There was belligerence in his manner I didn't care for. Anyway, he claimed to know Anne Van Lier's whereabouts. Whether he'd visited her he didn't say. He wanted to know who the other women are. Pressing me for information. I said I couldn't help him. Then, last night as I've said, someone very resourceful somehow plucked that very information from our computer files." He gestured a little awkwardly, denying personal responsibility. There was no such thing as totally secure in a world managed by machines. "I thought John ought to know."

Taja's eyes were unwinking in her odd, scarily immobile face for a few moments longer. Then she abruptly quit the foyer, moving soundlessly on slippered feet, leaving the sharp scent of her perfume behind—perfume that didn't beguile, it mugged you. She disappeared down a hallway lined with a dozen hugely valuable portraits and drawings by Old Masters.

Mellichamp licked his lips and waited, hat in hand, feeling obscurely humiliated. He heard no sound other than the slight wheeze of his own breath within the apartment.

"I, I really must be going," he said to a bust of Hadrian and his own backup reflection in a framed mirror that once had flattered royalty in a Bavarian palace. But he waited another minute before opening one of the bronze doors and letting himself out into the elevator foyer.

Gypsy whore, he thought again, extracting some small satisfaction from this judgment. Fortunately he seldom had to deal with her. Just to lay eyes on the Woman in Black with her bilious temperament and air of closely held violence made him feel less secure in the world of social distinction that, beginning with John Ransome's money, he had established for himself: a magical, intoxicating, uniquely New York place where money was in the air always, like pixie dust further enchanting the blessed.

Money and prestige were both highly combustible, however. In circumstances such as a morbid scandal could arrange, disastrous events turned reputations to ash.

The elevator arrived.

Not that he was legally culpable, Cy assured himself while descending. It had become his mantra. On the snowy bright-eyed street he headed for his limo at the curb, taking full breaths of the heady winter air. Feeling psychologically exonerated as well, blamelessly distanced from the tragedy he now accepted must be played out for the innocent and guilty alike.

Peter O'Neill arrived in Las Vegas on an early flight and signed for his rental car in the cavernous baggage claim area of McCarran airport.

"Do you know how I can find a place called the King Rooster?"

The girl waiting on him hesitated, smiled ironically, looked up and said softly, "Now I wouldn't have thought you were the type."

"What's that mean?"

"First trip to Vegas?"

"Yeah."

She shrugged. "You didn't know that the King Rooster is, um, a brothel?"

"No kidding?"

"They're not legal in Las Vegas or Clark County." She looked thoughtfully at him. "If you don't mind my saying—you probably could do better for yourself. But it's none of my business, is it?" She had two impish dimples in her left cheek.

Next, Peter thought, she was going to tell him what time she got off from work. He smiled and showed his gold shield.

"I'm not on vacation."

"Ohhh. *NYPD Blue*, huh? I hated it when Jimmy Smits died." She turned around the book of maps the car company gave away and made notations on the top sheet with her pen. "When you leave the airport, take the interstate south to exit thirty-three, that's

Route 160 west? Blue Diamond Road. You
want to go about forty miles past Blue Diamond to Nye County. When you get there
you'll see this big mailbox on the left with a
humungous, um, red cock—the crowing
kind—on top of it. That's all, no sign or anything. Are you out here on a big case?"

"Too soon to tell," Peter said.

The whorehouse, when he got there, wasn't
much to look at. The style right out of an
old Western movie: two square stories of
cedar with a long deep balcony on three
sides. In the yard that was dominated by a
big cottonwood tree the kind of discards
you might see at a flea market were scattered around. Old wagon wheels, an art-
glass birdbath, a dusty carriage in the
lean-to of a blacksmith's shed. There was a
roofed wishing well beside the flagstone
walk to the house. A chain-link fence that
clashed with the rustic ambience sur-
rounded the property. The gate was locked;
he had to be buzzed in.

Inside it was cool and dim and New Or-
leans rococo, with paintings of reclining

nudes that observed the civilities of fin de siècle. Nothing explicit to threaten a timid male; their pussies were as chaste as closed prayer books. A Hispanic maid showed Peter into a separate parlor. Drapes were drawn. The maid withdrew, closing pocket doors. Peter waited, turning the pages of an expensive-looking leather-bound book featuring porn etchings in a time of derbies and bustles. The maid returned with a silver tray, delicate china cups and coffee service.

She said, "You ask for Eileen. But she is indispose this morning. There is another girl she believe you will like, coming in just a—"

Peter flashed his shield and said, "Get Eileen in here. Now."

Ten more minutes passed. Peter opened the drapes and looked at sere mountains, the mid-range landscape pocked and rocky. A couple of wild burros were keeping each other company out there. He drank coffee. The doors opened again. He turned.

She was tall, a little taller than Peter in her high heels. She wore pale green silk lounging pajamas and a pale green harem mask that clung to the contours of her face but revealed only her eyes: they were dark, plummy, febrile in pockets of mascara. Tiny moons of sclera showed beneath the pupils.

"I'm Eileen."

"Peter O'Neill."

"Is there a problem?"

"What's with the mask, Eileen?"

"That's why you asked for me, isn't it? All part of the show you want."

"No. I didn't know about—. Mind taking the mask off?"

"But that's for upstairs," she protested, her tone demure. She began running her hands over her breasts, molding the almost sheer material of the draped pajamas around dark nipples. She cupped her breasts, making of them an offering.

"Listen, I didn't come here to fuck you. *Just take it off.* I have to see—what that bastard did to you, Eileen."

Her hands fell to her sides as she exhaled; the right hand twitched. Otherwise she didn't move.

"You *know?* After all these years I'm going to find out who did this to me?"

"I've got a good idea."

She made a sound deep in her throat of pain and sorrow, but didn't attempt to remove the mask. She shied when Peter impatiently put out a hand to her shrouded face.

"It's okay. You can trust me, Eileen." Inches from her body, feeling the heat of her, aware of a light perfume and arousing musk, he reached slowly behind her blond head and touched the little bow where her mask was tied as gently as if he were about to grasp a butterfly.

"I've only trusted one man in my life," she said dispiritedly. Then, unagressively but firmly, she snugged her groin against his, tamely laying her head on his shoulder so he could easily untie the mask.

He'd been expecting scars similar to those Anne Van Lier wore for life. But Eileen's were worse. Much of her face had burned, rendered almost to bone. The scar gullies were slick and mahogany-colored, with glisters of purple. He could see a gleam of her back teeth on the left, most heavily damaged side.

She flinched at his appalled examination, lowering her head, thrusting at him with her pelvis.

"All right," she said. "Now you're satisfied? Or are we just getting started?"

"I told you I didn't want to—"

"That's a lie. You're ready to explode in your pants." But she relented, stepping back from him, with a grin that was almost evil in the context of a ravaged face. "What's the matter? Your mommy told you to stay away from women like me? I'm clean. Cleaner than any little piece you're likely to pick up in a bar on Friday night. Huh? We're regulated in Nevada, in case you didn't know. The Board of Health dudes are here every week."

"I just want to talk. How did you get the face, Eileen?"

Her breath whistled painfully between her teeth.

"Fuck you mean? It's all in the case file."

"But I want to hear it from you."

Her face had little mobility, but her lovely eyes could sneer.

"Oh. Cops and their perversions. You all belong in a Dumpster. Give me back my mask."

She shied again when he tried to tie the mask on, then sighed, touching one of Peter's wrists, an exchange of intimacy.

"My face, my fortune," she said. "Would you believe how many men need a freakshow to get them up? God damn all of them. Present company excluded, I guess. You try to act tough but you've got a kind face." With the mask secure she felt bold enough to look him in the eye. "Your coffee must have cooled off by now," she said, suddenly the gracious hostess. "Would you like another cup?"

He nodded. She sat on the edge of a gilt and maroon–striped settee to pour coffee for them.

"So you want to hear it again. Why not?" She licked a sugar cube a couple of times before putting it into her cup. "I was alone in the lab, working on an experiment. Part of my PhD requirement in O-chem." Peter sipped coffee from the cup she handed him as he remained standing close to the settee. Still encouraging the intimacy she seemed to crave. It wasn't just cop technique to get someone to spill their guts. He felt anguish for Eileen, as her eyes wandered in remembrance. "I, I was tired, you know, hadn't slept for thirty-six hours. Something like that. Didn't hear anyone come in. Didn't know he was there until he was breathing down my neck." She looked up. "Is this what turns you on?" she said, as if she'd lost track of who he was. Only another john to be entertained.

She took Peter's free hand, raised it to her face, guided his ring finger beneath the mask and between her lips, touching it with the tip of her tongue. That was a new one on Peter, but the effect was disturbingly erotic.

"I started to turn on my stool," Eileen said, her voice close to a whisper as she looked up at Peter, lips caressing his captive finger, "and got a cup of H_2SO_4 in my face."

"But you didn't see—"

"All I saw was a gloved hand, an arm. Then—I was burning in hell." She bit down on his finger, at the base of the nail, laughed delightedly when he jerked his hand away.

"I can tell you who it was," Peter said angrily. "Because you're not the first woman who posed for John Ransome and got a face like yours."

He wasn't fully prepared for the ferocity with which she came at him, hissing like a feral cat, hands clawlike to ream out his eyes. He caught her wrists and forced her hands down.

"John Ransome? That's crazy! John loved me and I loved him!"

"Take it easy, Eileen! Did he come to see you after it happened?"

"No! So what? You think I wanted him to

see me like this? Think I want anyone looking at me unless they're paying for it? Oh
how I make them pay!"

"Eileen, I'm sorry." He had used as much
force as he dared; she was strong in her fury
and could inadvertantly break a wrist struggling with him. When she was off balance Peter pushed her hard away from him. "I'm
sorry, but I'm not wrong." He moved later-
ally away from her, not wanting some of his
face to wind up under her fingernails. But
she had choked on her outrage and was having trouble getting her breath.

"F-Fuck you! What are you cops . . . trying
to *do* to John? Did one of the others say
something against him? Tell me, I'll tear her
fucking heart out!"

"Were you that much in love with him?"

"I'm not talking to you anymore! Some
things are still sacred to me!"

Eileen backed up a few steps and sat down
heavily, her body in a bind as if she wore a
straitjacket, harrowing sounds of grief in her
throat.

"Whatever happened to that PhD?" he
asked calmly, though the skin of his forearms was prickling.

"That was someone else. Get out of here, before I have you thrown out. The sheriff and I are old friends. We paint each other's toenails. The chain-link fence? The goddamn desert? Forget about it. This is my *home*, no matter what you think. I *own* the Rooster. John paid for it."

Saying his name she quaked as if an old, unendurable torment was about to erupt. She leaned forward and, one arm moving jerkily like a string puppet's, she began smashing teacups on the tray with her fist. Shards flew. When she stopped her hand was bleeding profusely. She put it in her lap and let it bleed.

"On your way, bud," Eileen said to Peter. "Would you mind asking Lourdes to come in? I think it may be time for my meds."

While he was waiting at the Las Vegas airport for his flight to Houston, delayed an hour and a half because of a storm out of the Gulf of Mexico, Peter composed a long e-mail to Echo, concluding with:

So far I can't prove anything. There's at least two more of them I need to see, so I'm on my way to Texas. But I want you to get off the island *now*. No good-byes, don't bother to

pack. Go to my Uncle Charlie's in Brookline.
3074 East Mather. Wait for me there, I'll only
be a couple of days.

By the time he boarded his flight to Hous-
ton, there still was no acknowledgment from
Echo. It was six thirty-six P.M. on the East
Coast.

John Ransome was still working in his aerie
studio and Echo was taking a shower when
the Woman in Black walked into Echo's bedroom without a knock and had a look
around. Art books heaped on the writing
desk. The blouse and skirt and pearls she'd
laid out for a leisurely dinner with Ransome.
Her silver rosary, her Bible, her laptop.
There was an e-mail message on the screen
from Rosemay, apparently only half-read.
Taja scrolled past it to another e-mail from a
girl whom she knew had been Echo's college roommate. She skipped that one too
and came to Peter O'Neill's most recent
message.

This one Taja read carefully. Obviously
Echo hadn't seen it, or she wouldn't have

been humming so contentedly in the slow-running shower, washing her hair.

Taja deleted the message. But of course if Peter didn't hear from Echo soon, he'd just send another, more urgent e-mail. The weather was decent for now, the Wi-Fi signal steady.

She figured she had four or five minutes, at least, to disable the laptop skillfully enough so that Echo wouldn't catch on that it had been sabotaged.

But Peter O'Neill was the real problem—just as she had suspected and conveyed to John Ransome in the beginning, when Ransome was considering Echo as his next subject.

No matter how he rated as a detective, he wasn't going to learn anything useful in Texas. Taja could be certain of that.

And she had a good idea of where he would show up during the next forty-eight hours.

TEN

"Eventually they would have reconstructed her face," the late Nan McLaren's aunt Elisa said to Peter. "The plastic surgery group is the best in Houston. World-renowned, in fact."

He was sitting with the aging socialite, who still retained a certain gleam that diet and exercise afforded septuagenarians, in the orangerie of a very large estate home in Sherwood Forest. There was a slow drip of rain from two big magnolias outside that were strung with tiny twinkling holiday lights. The woman had finished a brandy and soda and wanted another; she signaled the black houseboy tending bar. Peter declined another ginger ale.

"Of course Nan would never have looked the same. What was indefinable yet unique about her youthful beauty—gone forever. Her nose demolished; facial bones not just broken but shattered. Such unexpected cruelty, so deadly to the soul, destroyed her optimism, her innocent ecstasy and joie de vivre. If you're familiar with the portraits that John Ransome painted, you know the Nan I'm speaking of."

"I saw them on the Internet."

"I only wish the family owned one. I understand all of his work has increased tremendously in value in the past few years." Elisa sighed and shifted the weight of the bichon frise dog on her lap. She stared at a recessed gas log fire in one angle of the octagonal garden room. "Who would have thought that a single, unexpected blow from a man's fist could do such terrible damage?"

"In New York they're called 'sly-rappers,'" Peter said. "Sometimes they use a brick, or wear brass knuckles. They come up behind their intended victims, usually on a crowded sidewalk, tap them on a shoulder. And when they turn, totally defenseless, to see who's there—"

"Is it always a woman?"

"In my experience. Young and beautiful, like Nan was."

"Dreadful."

"I understand Houston PD didn't get anywhere trying to find the perp."

"'Perp?' Yes, that's how they kept referring to him. But it happened so quickly; there were only a couple of witnesses, and he disappeared while Nan was bleeding there on the sidewalk." She reached up for the drink that the houseboy brought her. "Her skull was fractured when she fell. She didn't regain consciousness for more than a week." Elisa looked at Peter while the bichon frise eagerly lapped at the brimming drink she held on one knee. "But you haven't explained why the New York police department is interested in Nan's case."

"I can't say at this time, I'm sorry. Could you tell me when Nan started doing heroin?"

"Between, I think, her third and fourth surgeries. What she really needed was therapy, but she stopped seeing her psychiatrist when she took up with a rather dubious young man. He, I'm sure, was the one who—what is the expression? Got her hooked."

"Calvin Cotrona. A few busts, petty stuff. Yeah, he was a user."

Elisa took her brandy and soda away from the white dog with the large ruff of a head; he scolded her with a sharp bark. "Can't give him any more," she explained to Peter. "He becomes obstreperous, and pees on the Aubusson. Rather like my third husband, who couldn't hold his liquor either. Quiet down, Richelieu, or mommy will become deeply annoyed." She studied Peter again. "You seem to know so much about Nan's tragedy and how she died. What is it you hoped to learn from me, Detective?"

Peter rubbed tired eyes. "I wanted to know if Nan saw or heard from John Ransome once she'd finished posing for him."

"Not to my knowledge. After she returned to Houston she was quite blue and unsociable for many months. I suspected at the time she was infatuated with the man. But I never asked. Is it important?" Elisa raised her glass but didn't drink; her hand trembled. She looked startled. "But you can't mean—you can't be thinking—"

"Mrs. McLaren, I've talked to two of Ransome's other models in the past few weeks. Both were disfigured. A knife in one case, sulphuric acid in the other. In a day or two, with luck, I'll be talking to another of the Ransome women, Valerie Angelus. And I hope to God that nothing has happened to *her* face because that's stretching coincidence way too far. And already it's scaring the hell out of me."

In his room at a Motel 6 near Houston's major airport, named for one of the U.S. presidents who had bloomed and thrived where a stink of corruption was part of the land, Peter called his Uncle Charlie in Brookline, Massachusetts. Thirty-six hours had passed since he'd e-mailed Echo from Vegas, but she hadn't showed up there. He tried Rosemay in New York; she hadn't heard from Echo either. He sent another e-mail that didn't go through. In exasperation he tried leaving a message on her pager, but it was turned off.

Frustrated, he stretched out on the bed with a cold washcloth over his eyes. Traveling always gave him a queasy stomach and a headache. He chewed a Pepcid and tried to convince himself he had nothing to seriously worry about. The other Ransome women he knew of or had already interviewed had been attacked months after their commitments to the artist, and presumably their love affairs, were over.

Violent psychopaths had consistent profiles. Pete couldn't see the urbane Mr. Ransome as a part-time stalker and slasher, no matter what the full moon could do to potentially unstable psyches. But there was another breed, and not so rare according to his readings of case studies in psychopathology, who, insulated by wealth and position and perverse beyond human ken, would pay handsomely to have others gratify their sick, secret urges.

There was no label he could pin on John Ransome yet. But the notion that Ransome had spent several weeks already carefully and unhurriedly manipulating Echo, first to seduce and finally to destroy her, detonated the fast-food meal that had been sitting undigested in his stomach like a bomb. He went into the bathroom to throw up, afterward sat on the floor exhausting himself in a helpless rage. Feeling Echo on his skin, allure of a supple body, her creases and small breast buds and tempting, half-awake eyes. Thinking of her desire to make love to him at the cottage in Bedford and his stiff-necked refusal of her. A defining instance of false pride that might have sent his life careering off in a direction he'd never intended it to go.

He wanted Echo now, desperately. But while he was savagely getting himself off what he felt was a whore's welcome in silk, what he saw was the rancor in Eileen's dark eyes.

———

John Ransome didn't show up at the house until a quarter of ten, still wearing his work clothes that retained the pungency of the studio. Oil paints. To Echo the most intoxicating of odors. She caught a whiff of the oils before she saw him reflected in the glass of one of the bookcases in the first-floor library where she had passed the time with a sketchbook and her Prismacolor pencils, copying an early Ransome seascape. Painting the sea gave her a lot of trouble; it changed with the swiftness of a dream.

"I am so sorry, Mary Catherine." He had the look of a man wearied but satisfied after a fulfilling day.

"Don't worry, John. But I don't know about dinner."

"Ciera's used to my lateness. I need twenty minutes. You could select the wine. Chateau Petrus."

"John?"

"Yes?"

"I was looking at your self-portrait again—"

"Oh, that. An exercise in monomania. But I was sick of staring at myself before I finished. I don't know how Courbet could have done *eight* self-studies. Needless to say he was better looking than I am. I ought to take that blunder down and shove it in the closet under the stairs."

"Don't you dare! John, really, it's magnificent."

"Well, then. If you like it so much, Mary Catherine, it's yours."

"What? No," she protested, laughing. "I only wanted to ask you about the girl—the one who's reflected in the mirror behind your chair? So mysterious. Who is she?"

He came into the library and stood beside her, rubbed a cheekbone where his skin, sensitive to paint-thinner, was inflamed.

"My cousin Brigid. She was the first Ransome girl."

"No, really?"

"Years before I began to dedicate myself to portraits, I did a nude study of Brigid. After we were both satisfied with the work, we burned it together. In fact, we toasted marshmallows over the fire."

Echo smiled in patient disbelief.

"If the painting was so good . . ."

"Oh, I think it was. But Brigid wasn't of age when she posed."

"And you were?"

"Nineteen." He shrugged and made a palms-up gesture. "She was very mature for her years. But it would have been a scandal. Very hard on Brigid, although I didn't care what anyone would think."

"Did you ever paint her again?"

"No. She died not long after our little bonfire. Contracted septicemia at her boarding school in Davos." He took a step closer to the portrait as if to examine the mirror-cameo more closely. "She had been dead almost two years when I attempted this painting. I missed Brigid. I included her as a—I suppose your term would be guardian angel. I did feel her spirit around me at the time, her wonderful, free spirit. I was tortured. I suppose even angels can lose hope for those they try to protect."

"Tortured? Why?"

"I said that she died of septicemia. The result of a classmate's foolhardy try at aborting Brigid's four-month-old fetus. And, yes, the child was mine. Does that disgust you?"

After a couple of blinks Echo said, "Nothing human disgusts me."

"We made love after we ate our marshmallows, shedding little flakes of burnt canvas as we undressed each other. It was a warm summer night." His eyes had closed, not peacefully. "Warm night, star bright. I remember how sticky our lips were from the marshmallows. And how beautifully composed Brigid seemed to me, kneeling. On that first night of the one brief idyll of our lives."

"Did you know about the baby?"

"Brigid wrote to me. She sounded almost casual about her pregnancy. She said she would take care of it, I shouldn't worry." For an instant his eyes seemed to turn ashen from self-loathing. "Women have always given me the benefit of the doubt, it seems."

"You're not convincing either of us that you deserve to suffer. You were immature, that's all. Pardon me, but shit happens. There's still hope for all of us, on either side of heaven."

While she was looking for a bottle of the Chateau Petrus '82 that Ransome had suggested they have with their dinner, Echo heard Ciera talking to someone. She opened another door between the rock-walled wine storage pantry and the kitchen and saw Taja sitting at the counter with a mug of coffee in her hands. Echo smiled but Taja only stared before deliberately looking away.

"Oh, she comes and goes," Ransome said of Taja after Ciera had served their bisque and returned to the kitchen.

"Why doesn't she have dinner with us?" Echo said.

"It's late. I assume she's already eaten."

"Is she staying here tonight?"

"She prefers being aboard the boat if we're not in for a blow."

Echo sampled her soup. "She chose me for you—didn't she? But I don't think she likes me at all."

"It isn't what you're thinking."

"I don't know what I'm thinking. I get that way sometimes."

"I'll have her stay away from the house while you're—"

"No, please! Then I really am at fault somehow." Echo sat back in her chair, trailing a finger along the tablecloth crewelwork. "You've known her longer than all of the Ransome women. Did you ever paint Taja? Or did you toast marshmallows over those ashes too?"

"It would be like trying to paint a mask within a mask," Ransome said regretfully. "I can't paint such a depth of solitude. Sometimes . . . she's like a dark ghost to me, sealed in a world of night I'm at a loss to imagine. Taja has always known that I can't paint her." He had bowed his head, as if to conceal a play of emotion in his eyes. "She understands."

Eleven

The Knowles-Rembar Clinic, an upscale facility for the treatment of well-heeled patients with a variety of addictions or emotional traumas, was located in a Boston suburb not far from the campus of Wellesley College. Knowles-Rembar had its own campus of gracefully rolling lawns, brick-paved walks, great oaks and hollies and cedars and old rhododendrons that would be bountifully ablaze by late spring. In mid-December they were crusted with ice and snow. At one-twenty in the afternoon the sun was barely there, a mild buzz of light in layered gray clouds that promised more snow.

The staff psychiatrist Peter had come to see was a height-disadvantaged man who greatly resembled Barney Rubble with thick glasses. His name was Mark Gosden. He liked to eat his lunch outdoors, weather permitting. Peter accommodated him. He drank vending machine coffee and shared one of the oatmeal cookies Gosden's mother had baked for him. Peter didn't ask if the psychiatrist still lived with her.

"This is a voluntary facility," Gosden explained. "Valerie's most recent stay was for five months. Although I felt it was contrary to her best interests, she left us three weeks ago."

"Who was paying her bills?"

"I only know that they went to an address in New York, and checks were remitted promptly."

"How many times has Valerie been here?"

"The last was her fourth visit."

Peter was aware of a young woman slipping up on them from behind. She gave Peter a glance, put a finger to her lips, then pointed at Gosden and smiled mischievously. Mittens attached to the cuffs of her parka dangled.

She had a superb small face and jug-handle ears. In spite of the smile he saw in her eyes the blankness of a saintly disorder.

"And you don't think much of her chances of surviving on the outside," Peter said to the psychiatrist, who grimaced slightly.

"I couldn't discuss that with you, Detective."

"Do you know where I can find Valerie?"

Gosden brushed bread crumbs from his lap and drank some consommé from his lunchbox thermos. "Well, again. That's highly confidential without, of course, a court order."

When he put the thermos down the young woman, probably still a teenager Peter thought, put her chilly hands over Gosden's eyes. He flinched, then forced a smile.

"I wonder who this could be? I know! Britney Spears."

The girl took her hands away. "Ta-da!" She pirouetted for them, mittens flopping, and looked speculatively at Peter.

"How about that?" Gosden said. "It's Sydney Nova!" He glanced at his watch and said with a show of dismay, "Sydney, wouldn't you know it, I'm running late. 'Fraid I don't have time for a song today." He closed his lunchbox and got up from the bench, glancing at Peter. "If you'll excuse me, I do have a semi-nar with our psych-tech trainees. I'm sorry I can't be of more help."

"Thanks for your time, Doctor."

Sydney Nova leaned on the back of the bench as Gosden walked away, giving her hair a couple of tosses like a frisky colt.

"You don't have to run off, do you?" she said to Peter. "I heard what, I mean who, you and Goz were talking about."

"Did you know Valerie Angelus?"

Sydney held up two joined fingers, indicat-ing the closeness of their relationship. "When she's around, I mean. Do you have a cigarette I can bum?"

"Don't smoke."

"Got a name?"

"Peter."

"Cop, huh? You're yummy for a cop, Pete."

"Thanks. I guess."

Sydney had a way of whistling softly as a space filler. She continued to look Peter over.

"Yeah, Val and I talk a lot when she's here. She trusts me. We tell each other our dirty little secrets. Did you know she was a famous model before she threw a wheel the first time?"

"Yeah. I knew that."

"Say, dude. Do you like your father?"

"Sure. I like him a lot."

Sydney whistled again a little mournfully. She cocked her head this way and that, as if she were watching rats racing around her mental attic.

"Magazine covers when she was sixteen. Totally demento at eighteen. I guess fame isn't all that it's cracked up to be." Sydney cocked her head again, making a wry mouth. "But nothing beats it for bringing in the money." Whistling. "I haven't had my fifteen minutes yet. But I will. Keep getting sidetracked." She looked around the Knowles-Rembar campus, tight-lipped.

"Tell me more about Valerie."

"More? Well, she got like resurrected by that artist guy, spent a whole year with him on some island. Talk about head cases."

"You mean John Ransome?"

"You got it, delicious dude."

"What did he do to Valerie?"

"Some secrets you don't tell! I'll eat rat poison first. Oh, I forgot. Been there, done that. Hey, do you like *The Sound of Music*? I know all the songs."

As if she'd been asked to audition, Sydney stood on the bench with her little hands spread wide and sang some of "Climb Ev'ry Mountain." Peter smiled admiringly. Sydney did have a good voice. She basked in his attention, muffed a lyric, and stopped singing. She looked down at him.

"I bet I know where Val is. Most of the time."

"You do?"

"Help me down, Pete?"

He put his hands on her small waist. She contrived to collapse into his arms. In spite of the bulky parka and her boots she seemed to weigh next to nothing. Her parted lips were an inch from his.

"Val has a thing for cemeteries," Sydney said. "She can spend the whole day—you know, like it's Disneyland for dead people."

Peter set her down on the brick walk. "Cemeteries. For instance?"

"Oh, like that big one in Watertown? Mount Auburn, I think it is. Okay, your turn."

"For what, Sydney?"

"Whatever Gosden said about *voluntary*,

it's total bullshit. I'm in here like forever. But I could go with you. In the trunk of your car? Get me out of this place and I'll be real sweet to you."

"Sorry, Sydney."

She looked at him awhile longer, working on her lower lip with little fox teeth. Her gaze earthbound. She began to whistle plaintively.

"Thanks, Sydney. You were a big help."

She didn't look up as he walked away on the path.

"I put *my* father's eyes out," Peter heard her say. "So he couldn't find me in the dark anymore."

Peter spent a half hour in Mount Auburn cemetery, driving slowly in his rental car between groupings of very old mausoleums resembling grim little villages, before he came to a station wagon parked alongside the drive, its tailgate down. A woman in a dark veil was lifting an armload of flowers from the back of the wagon. He couldn't tell much about her by winter light, but the veil was an unfortunate clue. He parked twenty feet away and got out. She glanced his way. He didn't approach her.

"Valerie? Valerie Angelus?"

"What is it? I still have sites to visit, and I'm late today."

There were more floral tributes in the station wagon. But even from where he was the flowers didn't appear to be fresh; some were obviously withered.

"My name is Peter O'Neill. Okay if I talk to you, Valerie?"

"Could we just skip that, I'm very busy."

"I could help you while we talk."

She had started uphill in a swirl of large snowflakes toward a mausoleum of rust-red marble with a Greek porch. She paused and shifted the brass container of wilted sprays of flowers that she held in both arms and looked around.

"Oh. That would be very nice of you. What is the nature of your business?"

"I'm a New York City detective." He walked past the station wagon. She was waiting for him. "Are you in the floral business, Valerie?"

"No." She turned again to the mausoleum on the knoll. Peter caught up to her as she

was laying the memorial flowers at the vault's
entrance.

"Is this your family—"

"No," she said, kneeling to position the
brass pot just so in front of barred doors,
fussing with the floral arrangement. She
stepped back for a critical look at her work,
then glanced at the inscription tablet above
the doors. The letters and numerals were
worn, nearly unreadable. "I don't know who
they were," she said. "It's a very old mausoleum, as you can see. I suppose there
aren't many descendants who remember, or
care." She exhaled, the mourning veil flut-
tering. The veil did a decent job of disguis-
ing the fact that her facial features were
distorted. If the veil had been any darker or
more closely woven, probably she wouldn't
be able to see where she was going. "But
we'll all want to be remembered, won't we?"

"That's why you're doing this?"

"Yes." She turned and walked past him
down the knoll, boots crunching through
snow crust. "You're a detective? I thought
you might be another insurance investiga-
tor." The cold wind teased her veil. "Well,
come on. We're doing that one next." She

pointed to another vault across the drive from where she'd left her station wagon.

Peter helped her pull a white fan-shaped latticework filled with hothouse flowers onto the tailgate. The weather was too brutal for her not to be wearing gloves, but with her arm extended an inch or so of wrist was exposed. The multiple scars there were reminders of more than one suicide attempt.

They carried the lattice to the next mausoleum, large enough to enclose a family tree of Biblical proportions. A squirrel nickered at them from a pediment.

"They wouldn't pay, you know," Valerie said. "They claimed that because of my . . . history, I disabled my own car. Now that's just silly. I don't know anything about cars. How the brakes are supposed to work."

"Your brakes failed?"

"We'll put it here," Valerie said, sweeping away leaves collected in a niche. When she was satisfied that the tribute was properly displayed she looked uneasily around. "Next we're going to that sort of ugly one with the little fountain. But we need to hurry. They make me leave, you know, they're very strict about that. I can't come back until seven-thirty in the morning. So I . . . must spend the night by myself. That's always the hard part, isn't it? Getting through the night."

She didn't talk much while they finished unloading the flowers and dressing up the neglected mausoleums. Once she appeared to be pleased with her afternoon's work and at peace with herself, Peter asked, as if all along they'd been having a conversation about Ransome, "Did John come to see you after your accident?"

Valerie paused to run a gloved hand over a damaged marble plinth.

"Seventeen sixty-two. Wasn't *that* a long time ago."

"Valerie—"

"I don't know why you're asking me questions," she said crossly. "I'm cold. I want to go to my car." She began walking away, then hesitated. "John is . . . all right, isn't he?"

"Was the last time I saw him. By the way, he sends his warmest regards."

"Ohhh. Well, there's good news. I mean that he's all right. And still painting?" Peter nodded. "He's a genius, you know."

"I'm not one to judge."

Her tone changed as they walked on. "Let's just skip it. Talking about John. I can't get Silkie to shut up about him. He was always so generous to me. I don't know why Silkie is afraid of him. John wouldn't hurt her."

"Who's Silkie?"

"My friend. I mean she comes around. Says she's my friend."

"What does she say about John?"

Valerie closed the tailgate of her wagon. She crossed her arms, shuddering in spite of the fur-lined greatcoat she wore.

"That John wanted to—destroy all of us. So that only his paintings live. How ridiculous. The one thing I was always sure of was John's love for me. And I loved him. I'm able to say it now. *Loved* him. I was going to have his baby."

Peter took a few unhappy moments to absorb that. "Did he know?"

"Uh-uh. I found out after I left the island. I tried and tried to get in touch with John, but—*they* wouldn't let me. So I—"

Valerie faced Peter. In the twilight he could see her staring at him through the mesh over her face. She drew a horizontal line with a finger where her abdomen would be beneath the greatcoat.

"—Did this. And then I—" She held up an arm, exposing another scarred wrist above the fur cuff of the coat sleeve. "—did this. I was so . . . angry." She let her arm drop. "I don't know why I'm telling you this. But Dr. Gosden says 'Don't keep the bad things hidden, Valerie.' And you *are* a friend of John's. I would never want him to think poorly of me, as my mother used to say. Skip my mother. I never talk about her. Would you let John know I'm okay now? The anger is gone. I'll be just fine, no matter what Goz thinks." She lifted her face to the darkened sky, snowflakes spangling her veil. She swallowed nervously. "Do you have the time, Peter?"

"Ten to five." He stamped his feet; his toes were freezing.

"Gates close at five in winter. We'd better go."

"Valerie, when did Silkie pose for Ransome?"

"Oh, that was over with a year ago. I've never been jealous of her."

"Has Silkie had any accidents you know of?"

"No," Valerie said, sounding mildly perplexed. "But I told you, obsessing about John John *John* all the time has her in a state.

What I think, she's just having a hard time getting over him, so she makes up stuff about how he wants to hurt her. When it's the other way around. Goz would say she's having neurotic displacements. Anyway, she uses different names and doesn't have a home of her own. Picks up guys and stays with them a couple of nights, week at the most, then moves on."

"Then you don't know how I can get hold of her."

"Well—she left me a phone number. If I ever needed her, she said." Valerie turned the key in the ignition and the engine rumbled. She looked back at Peter. "I can try to find the number for you later." Her usually somber tone had lightened. "Why don't you come by, say, nine o'clock?"

"Where?"

"415 West Churchill. I'm in 6-A. I know I must seem old to you, Peter. Sometimes I feel—ancient. Like I'm living a whole lot of lives at the same time. Skip that. Truth is I'm only twenty-seven! You probably wouldn't have guessed. I'm not coming on to you or anything, but I could make dinner for us. Would you like that?"

"Very much. Thank you, Valerie."

"Call me Val, why don't you?" she said, and drove off.

Echo was rosy-fresh from a long hot soak, sitting at the foot of her bed with her hair bound up, frowning at the laptop computer she couldn't get to work. She looked up at a knock on her door; she was clearing her throat to speak when the door opened and John Ransome looked in.

"Oh, Mary Catherine. I'm sorry—"

"No, it's okay. I was about to get dressed. John, there's something wrong with my laptop, it isn't working at all."

He shook his head. "Wish I could help. I'm barely computer literate; I've never even looked inside one of those things. There's a computer in my office you're welcome to use."

"Thank you."

He was closing the door when she said, "John?"

"Yes?"

"It's going well for you, isn't it? Your paint-

ing. You know, you looked happy today—
well, most of the time."

"Did I?" he smiled, almost reluctant to
confirm this. "All I know is, the hours go by
so quickly in good company. And the work—
yes, I am pleased. I don't feel tired tonight.
How about you? Posing doesn't seem to tire
or bore you."

"Because I always have something interesting to think about or tell you. I try not to
talk *too* much. I'm not tired either but I'm
starving."

"Then I'll see you downstairs." But he
didn't leave or look away from her. He'd had
his own bath. He wore corduroys and a thick
sweater with a shawl collar. He had a glass of
wine in his left hand. "Mary Catherine, I was
thinking—but this really isn't the time, I'm
intruding."

"What is it, John? You can come in, it's okay."

He smiled and opened the door wider.
But he stayed in the doorway, drank some
wine, looked fondly at her.

"I've been thinking of trying something
new, for me. Painting you contrapposto,
nothing else on the canvas, no background."

She nodded thoughtfully.

"Old dog, new tricks," he said with a shrug, still smiling.

"You'd want me to pose nude, then."

"Yes. Unless you have strong reservations. I'd understand. It's just an idea."

"But I think it's a good idea," she said quickly. "You know I'm in favor of whatever makes the work go more easily, inspires you. That's why I'm here."

"You don't have to decide impetuously," he cautioned. "There's plenty of time—"

Echo nodded again. "I'm fine with it, John. Believe me."

After a few moments she rose slowly from the bed, her lips lightly compressed, with a certain inwardness that distanced her from Ransome. She slowly and with pleasure let down her hair, arms held high, glistening by lamplight. She gave her abundant dark mane a full shakeout, then stared at the floor for a few seconds longer before turning away from him as she undid the towel.

Ransome's face was impassive as he stared at Echo, his creative eye absorbing motion, light, shadow, coloring, contour. In that part

of his mind removed from her subtle eroti-
cism there was a great cold weight of ocean,
the tolling waves.

Having folded the towel and lain it on the
counterpane, Echo was still, seeming not to
breathe, a hand outstretched as if she were a
nymph reaching toward her reflection on
the surface of a pool.

When at last she faced him she was easeful
in her beauty, strong in her trust of herself,
her purpose, her value. Proud of what they
were creating together.

"Will you excuse me now, John?" she said.

TWELVE

When Valerie finished dressing for her anticipated dinner date with Peter O'Neill, having selected a clingy rose cocktail dress she'd
almost forgotten was in her closet and a veil
from her drawerful of veils to match, she returned to the apartment kitchen to check on
how dinner was coming along. They were
having gingered braised pork with apple and
winter squash kebobs. She'd marinated the

pork and other ingredients for two hours. The skewers were ready to grill as soon as Peter arrived. There was a bowl of tossed salad in the refrigerator. For dessert—now what had she planned for dessert? Oh, yes. Lemon-mint frappes.

But as soon as she walked into the small neat kitchen Valerie saw that the glass dish on the counter was empty and clean. No pork cubes marinating in garlic, orange juice, allspice, and olive oil. The unused metal skewers were to the left of the dish. The recipe book lay open.

She stared blankly at the untouched glass dish. Her scarred lips were pursed beneath her veil. She felt something let go in her mind and build momentum swiftly, like a roller-coaster on the downside of a bell curve with a 360-degree loop just ahead. She heard herself scream childishly on a distant day of fun and apprehension.

But I—

"There's nothing in the refrigerator either," she heard her mother say. "Just a carton of scummy old milk."

The roller-coaster plummeted into a pit of darkness. Valerie turned. Her mother was leaning in the kitchen doorway. The familiar sneer. Ida had compromised the ardor of numerous men (including Valerie's daddy), methodically breaking them on the wheel of her scorn. Now her once-lush body sagged; her potent beauty had turned, glistering like the scales of a dead fish.

"Hopeless. You're just hopeless, Valerie."

Valerie swallowed hurt feelings, knowing it was pointless to try to defend herself. She closed her eyes. The thunder of the roller-coaster had reached her heart. When she looked up again her mother was still hanging around with her wicked lip and punishing sarcasm. Giving it to little Val for possessing the beauty Ida had lost forever. Valerie could go deaf when she absolutely needed to. Now should she take a peek into the refrigerator? But she knew her mother had been right. Good intentions aside, Val accepted that she'd drifted off somewhere when she was supposed to be preparing a feast.

Okay, embarrassing. Skip all that.

Valerie returned to the dining nook where the table was set, the wine decanted, candles lit. Beautiful. At least she'd done that right. She was thirsty. She thought it

would be okay if she had a glass of wine before John arrived.

No, wait—could he really be coming to
see her after all this time? She glanced fear-
fully at her veiled reflection in the dark of
the window behind the table. Then she
picked up the carafe in both hands and managed to pour a glass nearly full without
spilling a drop. As she drank the roller-
coaster stopped its jolting spree, swooping
from brains to heart and back again.

Her mother said, "You can't be in any
more pageants if you're going to wet yourself onstage. We're all fed up, just fed up and
disgusted with you, Val."

Valerie looked guiltily at the carpet between her feet where she was dripping urine.
The roller-coaster gave a start-up lurch,
pitching her sideways. And she wasn't se-
curely locked in this time. She felt panic.

Her mother said, "For once have the guts
to take what's coming to you."

Valerie said, "You're an evil bitch and I've
always hated you."

Her mother said, "Fuck that. You hate
yourself."

No use arguing with her when Ida was in

high dander and fine acidic fettle. When she was death by a thousand tiny cuts.

Valerie felt the slow, heavy, ratcheting up of the coaster toward the pinnacle that no longer seemed unobtainable to her. Her throat had swelled nearly closed from unshed tears.

She set her glass down and filled it again. Walked a little unsteadily with the motion of the roller-coaster inside her providing impetus through the furnished apartment that was bizarrely decorated with old putrid flowers she picked up for nickels and dimes at the wholesale market. She unlocked the door and walked out, leaving the door standing open.

When the elevator came she wasn't at all surprised to see John Ransome inside.

"Where're you going?" he asked her. "To the top this time?"

"Of course."

He pushed the button for the twentieth floor. Valerie sipped her wine and stared at him. He looked the same. The smile that went down like cream and had you purring in no time. But that was then.

"You did love me, didn't you?" she asked timidly, barely hearing herself for the racket

the roller-coaster was making, all the scream-
ing souls aboard.

"Don't make me deal with that now," he
said, a hint of vexation souring his smile.

Valerie pushed the veil she'd been holding away from her face to the crown of her
head, where it became tangled in her hair.

"You were always an insensitive selfish son
of a bitch."

"Good for you, Valerie," her mother said.
Coming from Ida it was like a benediction.

John Ransome acknowledged her human
failings and with a ghostly nod forgave her.

"I believe this is your floor."

Valerie got off the elevator, kicked her
shoes from her feet (no good for walking on
walls) and proceeded to the steel door that
led to the roof of her building. There she
quailed.

"Isn't anyone coming with me?" she said.

When she turned around she saw that the
elevator was empty, the doors silently closing.

Oh, well, Valerie thought. *Skip it.*

Peter arrived at 415 West Churchill thirty
seconds behind the fire department—a

pumper truck and a paramedic bus—which had passed him on the way. Two police cars were just pulling up from different directions. Two couples with dogs on leashes were looking up at the roof of the high-rise building. The doorman apparently had just finished throwing up in shrubbery.

The night was windless. Snow fell straight down, thick as a theatre scrim. The dogs were agitated in the presence of death. The body lay on the walk about twenty feet outside the canopy at the building's entrance. Red dress contrasting with an icy, broken-off wing of an arborvitae. Pete knew who it was, had to be, before he got out of the car.

He checked his watch automatically. Eight minutes to nine o'clock. His stomach churned from shock and rage as he walked across the street and stepped over a low snowbank, shield in hand.

One of the cops was taking a tarp and body bag out of the trunk of his unit. The other one was talking to the severely shaken doorman.

"She just missed me." He looked at the front of his coat as if afraid of finding traces of spattered gore. "Hit that tree first and bounced." He looked around, face white as snails. "Aw Jesus."

"Any idea who she is?"

"Well, the veil. She always wore veils, you know, she was in an accident, went headfirst through the windshield. Valerie Angelus. Used to be a model. Big-time, I mean."

Peter kneeled beside Valerie's body, lying all wrong in its heaped brokenness. Twenty-one stories including the roof, a minimum of two hundred twenty feet. Her blood black on the recently cleared walk, absorbing snowflakes. The cop put his light on Valerie's head for a few seconds; fortunately not much of her face was showing. Peter told him to turn the flashlight off. He crossed himself and stood.

"Want I should check the roof?" the uniform asked him. "Before CSI gets here?"

Pete nodded. He was a couple of states outside of his jurisdiction and still on autopilot, trying to deal with another dead end of a long-running tragedy.

The paramedics had come over. Peter didn't want to explain his presence or interest in Valerie to the detectives who would be showing up along with CSI. Time to go.

When Peter turned away he saw a familiar face through the fall of snow. She was about a hundred feet away. She had stepped out on the driver's side of a Cadillac Escalade that was idling at an intersection. He knew her, but he couldn't place her.

She was tall, a black woman, well-dressed. Even at that distance an expression of horror was vivid on her face. He wondered how long she'd been there. He stared at her, but nothing clicked right away. Nevertheless he began walking briskly toward the woman.

His interest startled her. She slipped back into the Escalade.

Glimpsing her from a different angle, he remembered. She had been John Ransome's model before Echo. And as far as he could tell, although the snow obscured his vision, there was nothing wrong with her face.

Then she had to be Silkie, Valerie's friend. Who, Valerie had claimed, was afraid—very afraid—of John Ransome.

He began running toward the Escalade, shield in hand. But Silkie, after staring at him for a couple of moments through the windshield, looked back and threw the SUV into reverse. Hell-bent to get out of there. As if the shock of Valerie's death had been replaced by fear of being detained by cops and questioned.

Of all the Ransome women, she just might be the one who could help him nail John Ransome's ass. Pete ran. She couldn't drive backwards forever, even though she was pulling away from him.

At the next intersection she swerved around a car that had jammed on its brakes and slid to the curb. Obviously the Escalade was in four-wheel drive; no handling problems. She straightened out the SUV and gunned it. But Peter got a break as the headlights of the car she had nearly run up on the sidewalk shone on the license plate. Long enough for him to pick up most of the plate number. He stopped running and watched the SUV disappear down a divided street. He took out his ballpoint pen and jotted down the number of the Escalade. Missing a digit, probably, but that wouldn't be a problem.

He had Silkie. Unless, of course, the SUV was stolen.

The wind was high. Echo dreamed uneasily. She was naked in the cottage in Bedford. Going from room to room, desperate to talk to Peter. He wasn't there. None of the phones she tried were working. Forget about e-mail; her laptop was still down.

John Ransome was calling her. Angry that she'd left him before she finished posing. But she didn't want to be with him. His studio was filled with ugly birds. She'd never liked birds since a pigeon pecked her once while she was sitting on a bench at the Central Park Zoo. These were all black, like the Woman in Black. They screeched at her from their perches in the cage John had put her in. He painted her from outside the cage, using a long brush with a sable tip that stroked over her body like waves. She wasn't afraid of these waves, but she felt guilty because she liked it so much, trembling at the onset of that great rogue wave that was rolling erotically through her body. She tried to twist and turn away from the insidious strokes of his brush.

"No! What are you trying to do to us? You're not going anywhere!"

Echo sat straight up in bed, breathing hard at the crest of her sex dream. Then she sagged to one side, weak from vertigo. All but helpless. Her mouth and throat were dry. She lay quietly for a minute or so until her heartbeat subsided and strength crept back into her hands. Her reading lamp was on. She'd fallen asleep while reading *Villette*.

The wind outside moaned and that shutter was loose again. When she moved her body beneath the covers she could tell her sap had been running at the climax of her dream. She sighed and yawned, still spikey with nerves, turned to reach for a bottle of water on the night table and discovered John Ransome standing in the doorway of her bedroom.

He was unsteady on his feet, head nodding a little, eyes glass. Dead drunk, she thought, with a jolt of fear.

"John—"

His lips moved but he didn't make a sound.

"You can't be here," she said. "Please go away."

He leaned against the jamb momentarily, then walked as if he were wearing dungeon irons toward the bed.

"No, John," she said. Prepared to fight him off.

He gestured as if waving away her objection. "Couldn't stop her," he mumbled. "Hit me. Gone. This is—"

Three feet from Echo he lost what little control he had of his body, pitched forward to the bed, held onto the comforter for a few moments, eyes rolling up meekly in his head; then he slowly crumpled to the floor.

Echo jumped off the bed to kneel beside him. She saw the swelling lump as large as her fist through the hair on the left side of his head. There was a little blood—in his hair, sprinkled on his shirt collar. Not a gusher. She didn't mind the sight of blood but she knew she might have lost it if he was critically injured. Didn't look so bad on the outside but the fragile brain had taken a beating. That was her biggest worry. There was no doctor on the island. Three men and a woman were certified as EMTs, but Echo didn't know who they were or where they lived.

She was able to lift him up onto the bed. Déjà vu all over again, without the threat of hypothermia this time. He wasn't unconscious. She rolled him onto his stomach and turned his head aside so he would be less likely to aspirate his own vomit if he became nauseous. Ciera, she knew, sometimes got

the vapors over a hot stove and kept ammo-
nium carbonate on hand. Echo fled downstairs to the kitchen, found the smelling
salts, twisted ice in a towel and ran back to
her room.

She heard him snoring gently. It had to be
a good sign. She carefully packed the
swelling in ice.

What a crack on the head. Let him sleep
or keep him awake? She wiped at tears that
wouldn't stop. Go down the road and knock
on doors until she found an EMT? But she
was afraid to go out into freezing wind and
dark, afraid of Taja.

Taja, she thought, as the shutter slammed
and her backbone iced up to the roots of her
hair. Couldn't stop her, John had said. *Gone*.
But why had she done this to him, what were
they fighting about?

Echo slid the hammer from under the
bed. She went to the door. There was no
lock. She put a straight-back chair against it,
jammed under the doorknob, then climbed
back onto her bed beside John Ransome.

She counted his pulse, wrote it down,
noted the time. Every fifteen minutes. Keep
doing it, all night. While watching over him.

Until he woke up, or—but she refused to think about the alternative.

At dawn he stirred and opened his eyes. Looked at her without comprehension.

"Brigid?"

"I'm Ec—Mary Catherine, John."

"Oh." His eyes cleared a little. "Happened to me?"

"I think Taja hit you with something. No, don't touch that lump." She had him by the wrist.

"Wha? Never did that before." An expression close to terror crossed his face. "Where she?"

"I don't know, John."

"Bathroom."

"You're going to throw up?"

"No. Don't think so. Pee."

She helped him to her bathroom and waited outside in case he lost consciousness again and fell. She heard him splash water in his face, moaning softly. When he came out again he was steadier on his feet. He glanced at her.

"Did I call you Brigid?"

"Yes."

"Would've been like you, if she'd lived."

"Lie down again, John."

"Have to—"

"Do what?"

He shook his head, and regretted it. She guided him to her bed and he stretched out on his back, eyes closing.

"Stay with me?"

"I will, John." She touched her lips to his dry lips. Not exactly a kiss. And lay down beside him, staring at the first flush of sun through the window with the broken shutter. She felt anxious, a little demoralized, but immensely grateful that he seemed to be okay.

As for Taja, when he was ready they were going to have a serious talk. Because she understood now just how deeply afraid John Ransome was of the Woman in Black.

And his fear had become hers.

THIRTEEN

The SUV Silkie had been driving belonged to a thirty-two-year-old architect named Milgren who lived a few blocks from MIT in

Cambridge. Peter called Milgren's firm and was told he was attending a friend's wedding in the Bahamas and would be away for a few days. Was there a Mrs. Milgren? No.

Eight inches of fresh snow had fallen overnight. The street in front of the building where Milgren lived was being plowed. Peter had a late breakfast, then returned. The address was a recently renovated older building with a gated drive on one side and tenant parking behind it. He left his rental car in the street behind a painter's van. The day was sharply blue, with a lot of ice-sparkle in the leafless trees. The snow had moved west.

The gate of the parking drive was opening for a Volvo wagon. He went in that way and around to the parking lot, found the Cadillac Escalade in its assigned space. Apartment 4-C.

There were four apartments on the fourth floor, two at each end of a wide well-lit marble-floored hallway. There was a skylight above the central foyer: elevator on one side, staircase on the other.

The painter or painters had been working on the floor, but the scaffold that had been erected to make it easier to get at the fifteen-foot-high tray ceiling was unoccupied. On the scaffold a five-gallon can of paint was overturned. A pool of it like melted pistachio ice cream was spreading along the marble floor. The can still dripped.

Pete looked from the spilled paint to the door of 4-C, which stood open a couple of feet. There was a TV on inside, loudly showing a rerun of *Hollywood Squares.*

He walked to the door and looked in. An egg-crate set filled with decommissioned celebrities was on the LCD television screen at one end of a long living room. He edged the door half open. A man wearing a painter's cap occupied a recliner twenty feet from the TV. All Peter could see of him was the cap, and one hand gripping an arm of the chair as if he were about to be catapulted into space.

Peter rapped softly and spoke to him but the man didn't look around. There was a lull in the hilarity on TV as they went to commercial. He could hear the man breathing. Shallow, distressed breaths. Pete walked in and across the short hall, to the living room. Plantation-style shutters were closed. Only a couple of low-wattage bulbs glowed in widely separated wall sconces. All of the apartment was quite dark in contrast to the brilliant day outside.

"I'm looking for Silkie," he said to the man. "She's staying here, isn't she?"

No response. Peter paused a few feet to the left of the man in the leather recliner. His feet were up. His paint-stained coveralls had the look of impressionistic master-pieces. By TV light his jowly face looked sweaty. His chest rose and fell as he tried to drag more air into his lungs.

"You okay?"

The man rolled his eyes at Peter. The fin-gers of his left hand had left raw scratch marks all over the red leather armrest. His other hand was nearly buried in the pulpy mass above his belt. Pete smelled the blood.

"She—made me do it—talk to the lady—get her to—unlock the door. Help me. Can't move. Guts are—falling out. My daughter's coming home—for the holidays. Now I won't be here."

Peter's gun was in his hand before the man had said ten words. "Where are they?"

The painter had run out of time. He

sagged a little as his life ebbed away. His eyes remained open. There was a burst of laughter from the TV.

"Jesus and Mary," Pete whispered, then raised his voice to a shout. "Silkie, you okay? It's the police!"

With his other hand he dug out his cell phone, dialed without looking, identified himself.

"Do you want police, fire, or medical emergency?"

"Cops. Paramedics. I've got a dying man here."

He began his sweep of the apartment while he was still on the phone.

"Please stay on the line, Detective," the dispatcher said. "Help is on the way."

"I may need both hands," Peter said, and dropped the cell phone back into his pocket.

He kicked open a door to what appeared to be the architect's study and workroom. Enough light coming in here to show him at a glance the room was empty.

"Silkie!"

The master bed- and sitting room was at the end of the hall. Double doors, one standing open. As he approached along one wall,

Glock held high in both hands, he made out the shapes of furnishings because of a bathroom light shining beyond a four-poster bed draped with a gauzelike material.

Furniture was overturned in the sitting room. A fish tank had been shattered.

Pete edged around the foot of the Victorian bedstead and had a partial view of a seminude body facedown on the tiles. Black girl. There was broken glass from a mirror and a ribbon of blood.

"Silkie, answer me, what happened here?"

He was almost to the bathroom door when Silkie stirred, looked around blank-eyed, then tried to push herself up with both hands as she flooded with terror. Blood dripped from a long cut that started below her right eye and ran almost to the jawline.

"Is she gone?" Silkie gasped.

Peter read the shock in her widening eyes but was a split second late turning as Taja came off the bed, where she'd been lying amid a pile of pillows he hadn't paid enough attention to, and slashed at him with her stiletto.

He turned his wrist just enough so veins weren't severed but he lost his automatic. He backhanded her in the face with his other hand. Taja went down in a sprawl that she corrected almost instantly, cat-quick, and rushed him again with her knife ready to thrust, held close to her side. Her face looked as wooden as a ceremonial mask. She knew her business. He blocked an attempt she made to slash upward near his groin and across the femoral artery. She knew where he was most vulnerable and didn't try for the chest, where her blade could get hung up on the zipper of his leather jacket, or his throat, which was partially protected by a scarf. And Taja was in no hurry: she was between him and his only way out. Acrobatic in her moves, she feinted him in the direction she wanted him to go—which was back against the bed and into the mass of sheer drapery hanging there.

Pete heard Silkie scream but he was too busy to pay attention to her. The bed drapery clung to him like spiderweb as he struggled to free himself and avoid Taja. She slashed away methodically, the material beginning to glow red from his blood.

His gun fired. Deafening.

Taja flinched momentarily, then went into a crouch, turning away from Peter, finding

Silkie. She was standing just inside the bathroom, Peter's Glock 9 in both hands.

"Bitch." She fired again, range about eight feet. Taja jerked to one side. hesitated a second, glanced at Peter, who had fought his way out of the drapery. Then she sprang to the bedroom doors and vanished.

Pete slipped a hand inside his jacket where his side stung from a long caress of Taja's stiletto. A lot of blood on the hand when he looked at it. Holy Jesus. He looked at Silkie, who hadn't budged from the threshold of the bathroom nor lowered his gun. When he moved toward her she gave him a deeply suspicious look. She was nude to well below her navel. Blood dripped from her chin. She had beautifully modeled features even Echo might have envied. Pete coughed, waited suspensefully, but no blood had come up. He saw that the cut on Silkie's face could've been a lot worse, the flesh laid open. Part of it was just a scratch down across the cheekbone. A little deeper in the soft flesh near her mouth.

He had to pry his gun from Silkie's hands. His own hands were so bloody he nearly dropped the Glock. He no longer considered going after Taja. Shock had him by the back of the neck. He heard sirens before a rising teakettle hiss in his ears shut out the sound. His face dripped perspiration, but his skin was turning cold. He had to lean against the jamb, his face a few inches from the tall girl's breasts. My God but they were something.

"What's your name?" he asked Silkie.

She had the hiccups. "Ma-MacKENzie."

"I'm Peter. Peter O'Neill. We're old friends, Silkie. We dated in New York. I came up here for a visit. Can you remember that?"

"Y-yes. P-P-PETEr O'Neill. From New York."

"And you don't know who attacked you. Never saw her before. Got that?"

He looked her in the eye, wondering if they had a chance in hell of selling it. She looked back at him with a slight twitch of her head.

"Why?"

"Because Valerie Angelus is dead and you came close and that, *that* he does not get away with, don't care how much money. I want John Ransome. Want his ass all to myself until I'm ready to hand him over."

"But Taja—"

"Taja's just been doing the devil's work. That's what I believe now. *Help me*, Silkie."

She touched a finger to her chin, wiped a

drop of blood away. The wound had nearly stopped oozing.

"All right," she said, beginning to cry. "How bad am I?"

"Cut's not deep. You'll always be beautiful. Listen. Hear that? Medics. On the way up. Now I need to—" He began to slide to the floor at her feet. Shuddering. His tongue getting a little thick in his mouth. "Sit down before I uh pass out. Silkie, put something on. Now listen to me. Way you talk to cops is, keep it simple. Say it the same way every time. 'We met at a party. He's only a friend.' No details. It's details that trip you up if you're lying."

"You are—a friend," she said, kneeling, putting an arm around him for a few moments. Then she stood and reached for a robe hanging up behind the bathroom door.

"We'll get him, Silkie. You'll never be hurt again. Promise." Finding it hard to breathe now. He made himself smile at her. "We'll get the bastard."

When Echo woke up half the day was gone. So was John Ransome, from her bed.

She looked for him first in his own room. He'd been there, changed his clothes. She found Ciera in Ransome's study, straightening up after what appeared to have been a donnybrook. A lamp was broken. Dented metal shade; had Taja hit him with it? Ciera stared at Echo and shook her head worriedly.

"Do you know where John is?"

"No," Ciera said, talkative as ever.

The day had started clear but very cold; now thick clouds were moving in and the seas looked wild as Echo struggled to keep her balance on the long path to the lighthouse studio.

The shutters inside the studio were closed. Looking up as she drew closer, Echo couldn't tell if Ransome was up there.

She skipped the circular stairs and took the cabinet-size birdcage elevator that rose through a shaft of opaque glass to the studio seventy-five feet above ground level.

Inside some lights were on. John Ransome was leaning over his worktable, knotting twine on a wrapped canvas. Echo glanced at her portrait that remained unfinished on the large easel. How serene she looked. In contrast to the turmoil she was feeling now.

He'd heard the elevator. Knew she was there.

"John."

When he looked back he winced at the pain even that slow movement of his head caused him. The goose egg, what she could see of it, was a shocking violet color. She recognized raw anger in conjunction with his pain, although he didn't seem to be angry at her.

"Are you all right? Why didn't you wake me up?"

"You needed your sleep, Mary Catherine."

"What are you doing?" The teakettle on the hot plate had begun to wheeze. She took it off, looking at him, and prepared tea for both of them.

"Tying up some loose ends," he said. He cut twine with a pair of scissors. Then his hand lashed out as if the stifled anger had found a vent; a tall metal container of brushes was swept off his worktable. She couldn't be sure he'd done it on purpose. His movements were haphazard, they mimicked drunkenness although she saw no evidence in the studio that he'd been drinking.

"John, why don't you—I've made tea—"

"No, I have to get this down to the dock, make sure it's on the late boat."

"All right. But there's time, and I could do that for you."

He backed into his stool, sat down uneasily. She put his tea within reach, then stooped to gather up the scattered brushes.

"Don't do that!" he said. "Don't pick up after me."

She straightened, a few brushes in hand, and looked at him, lower lip folded between her teeth.

"I'm afraid," he said tautly, "that I've reached the point of diminished returns. I won't be painting any more."

"We haven't finished!"

"And I want you to leave the island. Be on that boat too, Mary Catherine."

"Why? What have I— you can't mean that, John!"

He glanced at her with an intake hiss of breath that scared her. His eyes looked feverish. "Exactly that. Leave. For your safety."

"My—? What has Taja done? Why were you fighting with her last night? Why are you afraid of her?"

"Done? Why, she's spent the past few years

hunting seven beautiful women after I had finished painting them."

"Hunting—?"

"Then she slashed, burned, maimed—*killed*, for all I know! And always she returned to me after the hunt, silently gloating. Now she's out there again, searching for Silkie MacKenzie."

"Dear *God.* Why?"

"Don't you understand? To make them pay, for all they've meant to me."

Echo had the odd feeling that she wasn't fully awake after all, that she just wanted to sink to the floor, curl up and go back to sleep. She couldn't look at his face another moment. She went hesitantly to a curved window, opened the shutters there and rested her cheek on insulated safety glass that could withstand hurricane winds. She stared at the brute pounding of the sea below, feeling the force of the waves in the shiver of glass, repeating the surge of her own heartbeats.

"How long have you known?"

"More than two years ago I became suspicious of what she might be doing during prolonged absences. I hired the Blackwelder Organization to investigate. What they came up with was horrifying, but still circumstantial."

"Did you really *want* proof?" Echo cried.

"Of course I did! And last night I finally received it, an e-mail from Australia. Where one of my former models—"

"Another victim?"

"Yes," Ransome said, his head down. "Her name is Aurora Leigh. She'd been in seclusion. But she was in adequate shape emotionally to identify Taja as her attacker from sketches I provided."

"Adequate shape emotionally," Echo repeated numbly. "Why did Taja hit you last night?"

"I confronted her with what I knew."

"Was she trying to kill you?"

"No. I don't think so. Just letting me know her business isn't finished yet."

"Oh Jesus and Mary! The police—did you call—"

"I called my lawyers this morning. They'll handle it. Taja will be stopped."

"But what if Taja's still here? You'll need—"

"Her boat's gone. She's not on the island."

"There are dozens of islands where she could be hiding!"

"I can take care of myself."

"Oh, *sure*," Echo said, bouncing the heel of her hand off her forehead as she began to pace.

"Don't be frightened. Just go back to New York. If there's even a remote possibility Taja will be free long enough to return to Kincairn—well then, Taja is, she's always been, my responsibility."

Echo paused, stared, caught her breath, alarmed by something ominous hanging around behind his words. "Why do you say that? You didn't make her what she is. That must have happened long before you met her, where—?"

"In Budapest."

"Doing what, mugging tourists?"

"When I first saw Taja," he said, his voice laboring, "she was drawing with chalk on the paving stones near the Karoly Krt gate. For what little money passersby were willing to throw her way." He raised his head slowly. "I don't know how old she was then; I don't know her age now. As I told you once, terrible things had been done to her. She was barefoot, her hair wild, her dress shabby." He smiled faintly at Echo. His lips were nearly bloodless. "Yes, I should have walked on by. But I was astounded by her talent. She drew wonderful, suffering, religious faces. They burned with fevers, the hungers of martyrdom. All of the faces washing away each time it rained, or scuffed underfoot by the heedless. But every day she would draw them again. Her knees, her elbows were scabbed. For hours she barely paused to look up from her work. Yet she knew I was there. And after a while it was my face she sought, my approval. Then, late one afternoon when it didn't rain, I—I followed her. Sensing that she was dangerous. But I've never wanted a tame affair. It's immolation I always seem to be after."

His smile showed a slightly crooked eye tooth Echo was more or less enamored with, a sly imperfection.

"Just how dangerous she was at that time became a matter of no great importance. You see, we may all be dangerous, Mary Catherine, depending on what is done to us."

"Oh, was the sex that good?" Echo said harshly, her face flaming.

"Sometimes sex isn't the necessary thing, depending on the nature of one's obsession."

Echo began, furiously, to sob. She turned again to the horizon, the darkening sea.

After a couple of minutes he said, "Mary Catherine—"

"You know I'm not going! I won't let you give up painting because of what Taja did! You're not going to send me away, John, you need me!"

"It's not in your power to get me to paint again."

"Oh, isn't it?" She wiped her leaky nose on the sleeve of her fisherman's sweater; hadn't done that in quite a few years. Then she pulled off the sweater, gave her head a shake, swirling her abundant hair. Ransome smiled cautiously when she looked at him again, began to stare him down. A look as old, as eternal as the sea below.

"We have to complete what we've started," Echo said reasonably. She moved closer to him, the better for him to see the fierceness of eye, the high flame of her own obsession. She swept a hand in the direction of her portrait on his easel. "Look, John. And look again! I'm not just a face on a sidewalk. I *matter*!"

She seized and kissed him, knowing that the pain in his sore head made it not particularly enjoyable; but that wasn't her reason just then for doing it.

"Okay?" she said mildly and took a step back, clasping hands at her waist. The pupil. The teacher. Who was who awaited clarification, perhaps the tumult and desperation of an affair now investing the air they breathed with the power of a blood oath.

"Oh, Mary Catherine—" he said despairingly.

"I asked you, *is it okay?* Do we go on from here? Where? When? What do we do now, John?"

He sighed, nodded slightly. That hurt too. He put a hand lightly to the bump on his head.

"You're a tough, wonderful kid. Your heart . . . is just so different than mine. That's what makes you valuable to me, Mary Catherine." He gravely touched her shoulder, tapping it twice, dropped his hand. "And now you've been warned."

She liked the touch, ignored his warning. "Shall I pick up the rest of those brushes that were spilled?"

After a long silence Ransome said, "I've always found salvation in my work. As you must know. I wonder, could that be why your god sent you to me?"

"We'll find out," Echo said.

Peter heard one of the detectives ask, "How close did she come to his liver?"

A woman, probably the ER doc who had been stitching him up, replied, "Too close to measure."

The other detective on the team, who had the flattened Southie nasal tone, said, "Irish luck. Okay if we talk to him now?"

"He's awake. The Demerol has him groggy."

They came into Peter's cubicle. The older detective, probably nudging retirement, had a paunch and an archaic crook of a nose like an old Roman in marble. The young one, but not that young—close to forty, Peter guessed—had red hair in cheerful disarray and hard-ass good looks the women probably went for like a guilty pleasure. Cynicism was a fixture in his face, like the indentations from long-ago acne.

He grinned at Peter. "How you doin', you lucky baastud?"

"Okay, I guess."

"Frank Tillery, Cambridge PD. This here is my Fathah Superior, Sal Tranca."

"Hiya."

"Hiya."

Peter wasn't taken in by their show of camaraderie. They didn't like what they had seen in the architect's apartment and they didn't like what they'd heard so far from Silkie. They didn't like him, either.

"Find the perp yet?" he said, taking the initiative.

Sal said, "Hasn't turned up. Found her blade in a can of paint. Seven inches, thin, what they call a stiletto in the old country."

Tillery leaned against a wall with folded arms and a lemon twist of a grin and said, "Pete, you mind tellin' us why you was trackin' a homicidal maniac in our town without so much as a courtesy call to us?"

"I'm not on the job. I was—looking for Silkie MacKenzie. Walked right into the play."

"What did you want with MacKenzie? I mean, if I'm not bein' too subtle here."

"Met her—in New York." His ribs were taped, and it was hard for him to breathe. "Like I told you at the scene, had some time off so I thought I'd look her up."

"Apparently she was already shacked up with one guy, owns the apartment," Sal said. "Airline ticket in your coat pocket tells us you flew in from Houston yesterday morning."

Peter said, "I got friends all over. On vacation, just hangin' out."

"Hell of a note," Tillery said. "Lookin' to chill, relax with some good-lookin' pussy, next thing you know you're in Mass General with eighty-four stitches."

"She was real good with that, what'a'ya call it, stiletto?"

Sal said, "So, Pete. Want to do your statement now, or later we come around after your nap? As a courtesy to a fellow shield. Who seems to be goddamn well connected where he comes from." Sal looked around as if for a place to spit.

"I'll come to you. How's Silkie?"

"Plastic surgeon looked at her already.

There's gonna be some scarring they can clean up easy."

"She say she knew the perp?"

Tillery and Tranca exchanged jaundiced glances. "About as well as you did," Sal said.

"Well, you enjoy that dark meat," Tillery said. He was on the way out when something occurred to him to ask. He turned to Peter with his cynical grin.

"How long you had your gold, Pete?"

"Nine months."

"Hey, congrats. Sal here, he's got twenty-one years on the job. Me, I got eleven."

"Yeah?" Peter said, closing his eyes.

"What Frank is gettin' at," Sal said dourly, "we can smell a crock of shit when it's right under our noses."

FOURTEEN

Echo was putting her clothes back on inside the privacy cubicle in John Ransome's studio when she heard the door close, heard him locking her in.

"John!"

The door was thick tempered glass. He

looked back at her tiredly as she emerged holding the sweater to her bare breasts and tugged at the door handle, not believing this.

"I'm sorry," he said. His voice was muffled by the thickness of the door. "When it's done—if it's done tonight—I'll be back for you."

"No! Let me out *now*!"

He shook his head slightly, then clattered down the iron staircase like a man in search of a nervous breakdown while Echo battled the door; still unwilling to believe that she was locked up until Ransome decided otherwise.

She glanced at the nude study he had begun, only a free-flowing sketch at this point but unmistakably Echo. She then demonstrated, at the top of her voice, how many obscene street oaths she'd picked up over the years.

But the harsh wind off a tumbled sea that caused her glass jail to shimmy on its high perch wailed louder than she could hope to.

Peter woke up with a start when Silkie MacKenzie put a hand on his shoulder. He felt sharp pain, then nausea before he could focus on her.

"Hello, Peter. It's Silkie."

He swallowed his distress, attempted a smile. The right side of her face was neatly bandaged. "How you doin'?"

"I'll be all right."

"What time is it, Silkie?"

She looked at her gold Piaget. "Twenty past three."

"Oh, Jesus." He licked dry lips. There was an IV hookup in the back of his left hand for fluids and antibiotics. But his mouth was parched. With his heavily wrapped right hand—how many times had Taja cut him?—he motioned for Silkie to lean her face close to his. "Talk to you," he whispered. "Not here. They may have left a device. Couldn't watch both of them all the time."

"Isn't that illegal?"

"Wouldn't be admissable in a courtroom. But they don't trust either of us, so they could be fishing—for an angle to use during an interrogation. Walk me to the bathroom."

She got him out of bed and supported him, rolling the IV pole with her other hand. He had Silkie come inside the bathroom with him. All the fluids they'd dripped into Peter had him desperate to pee. Silkie continued to hold his elbow for support and looked at a wall.

"Today wasn't the first time Taja came after you," Pete said.

"No. Five months ago I was in Los Angeles. I had a commercial, the first work my agent was able to get for me after I'd finished my assignment with John. But John didn't want me working, you see. My face all over telly. That would have destroyed the—the allure, the fascination, the mystery he works so hard to create and maintain."

"So keep the paintings, destroy the model. I've seen Anne Van Lier and Eileen Wendkos."

Silkie looked around at him; she was close enough for Peter to feel the tremor that ran through her body.

"Then I had a glimpse of Taja, at a restaurant opposite Sunset Plaza. She pretended not to notice me. But I—all of my life I've had premonitions. There was suddenly the darkest, angriest cloud I'd ever seen pressing down on Sunset Boulevard. So I ran for my life. Later I hired private detectives. I was very curious to know what had happened to my—my predecessors? I found out, as you did. And once I talked to Valerie, I understood what my sixth sense had always told me about John. I believe he may be insane."

"We have to get out of here. Now. I have a rental car if Cambridge PD didn't impound it. But I'm not sure how much driving I can do." He bumped her as he turned in their small space; weakness followed pain, and it worried him. "Silkie, help me pull this IV out of my hand, then bring the rest of my clothes to me."

"Where are we going?"

"The nearest airport to Kincairn Island is in Bangor, Maine."

"I don't think the weather is good up there."

"Then the sooner we leave, the better. Get my wallet and watch from the lockbox. Use my credit card to reserve two seats on the next flight Boston to Bangor."

"I'm not so sure I want to do that. I mean, go back there. I'm afraid, Peter."

"Please, Silkie! You gotta help me. My girl's on that island with that sick son of a bitch Ransome!"

————

The owner and chief pilot of Lola's Flying Service at Bangor airport was going over accounts in her office when Peter and Silkie walked in at ten minutes to eight. Snow particles were flying outside the hangar, and they had felt sharp enough to etch glass.

Lola was a large cockeyed jalopy of a woman, salty as Lot's wife. Peter explained his needs.

"Chopper the two a ya's down to Kincairn in this freakin' weather? Not if I hope to achieve my average life expectancy."

Peter produced his shield. Lola greeted that show of authority with a lopsided smile.

"I'm Born Again, honeybunch; and I surely would hate to miss the Rapture. Otherwise what's Born Again good for?"

Silkie said, "Please listen to me. We must get there. Something very bad is going to happen on the island tonight. I have a premonition."

Lola, looking vastly amused, said, "Bullshit."

"Her premonitions are very accurate," Peter said.

Lola looked them over again. The bandages and bruises.

"I had my tea leaves read once. They said I

shouldn't get involved with people who show up looking like the losers in a domestic disturbance competition." She picked up the remains of a ham on whole wheat from a takeout carton and polished it off in two bites.

Silkie patiently opened her tote and took out a very large roll of bills, half of which, she made it plain to Lola, were hundreds.

"On the other hand," Lola said, "you have any premonitions about what this little jaunt is gonna cost you?"

"Name your price," Silkie said calmly, and she began laying C-notes in the carton on top of a wilted lettuce leaf.

Echo's immediate needs were met by a chemical toilet; a small refrigerator that contained milk, a wedge of Jarlsburg, bottled water and white wine; and an electric heater that dispelled the worst of the cold after sundown. There was also a large sheepskin throw to wrap up in while she rocked herself in the only chair in John Ransome's studio. Physically she was fine. She had drunk the rest of an already-opened bottle of Cabernet

Sauvignon, ordinarily enough wine to put her soundly to sleep. But the wind that was hitting forty knots according to the gauge outside and her circumstances kept her alert and sober, with an aching heart and a sense of impending tragedy.

If it's done tonight, Ransome had said forebodingly. What did he know about Taja, and what was he planning?

Every few minutes, between decades of the rosary that went everywhere with her, Echo jumped up restlessly to pace the inner circumference of the studio, then stopped to peer through the shutters in the direction of the stone house three hundred yards away. She could make out only blurred lights through horizontal lashings of snow. She'd seen nothing of Ransome since his head had disappeared down the circular lighthouse stairs. She hadn't seen anyone except Ciera, who had left the house early, perhaps dismissed by Ransome. In twilight, on her way across the island, Ciera's path had brought her within two hundred feet of the Kincairn light. Echo had pounded on the glass, screamed at her, but Ciera never looked up.

She'd turned off the studio lights. After the

wine she had a lingering headache, more from stress than from drinking. The light hurt her eyes and made it more difficult to see anything outside. At full dark she relied on the glow from the heater and the red warning strobe atop the studio for illumination.

When she tired of walking in circles and trying to see through the fulminating storm, she slumped in the rocking chair with her feet tucked under her. She was past sulking, brooding, and prayer. It was time to get tough with herself. *You have a little problem, Mary C.? Solve it.*

That was when the pulse of the strobe overhead gave her an idea of how to begin.

On the way down from Bangor in the three-passenger Eurocopter that had become surplus when Manuel Noriega fell out of favor with the CIA, Peter had plenty of time to reflect on the reasons why he'd never taken up flying as a hobby.

It was a strange night, clearing up in places on the coast but still with force eight winds. The sea from twelve hundred feet was visible to the horizon; beneath them it was a scumble of whitecaps going every which way. The sky overhead was tarnished silver in the light from the moon. Lola, dealing with the complexities of flying through the gauntlet of a gale that had the chopper rattling and vibrating, looked unperturbed, confident of her skills, although she was having a hard chew on the wad of grape-flavored gum in her right cheek.

"Should've calmed down some by now," she groused. "That's why we waited."

Silkie had become sick to her stomach two minutes after they lifted off at twelve-thirty in the morning, and she'd stayed sick and moaning all the way. Peter, whose father and uncles had always owned boats, was a competent sailor himself and used to rough weather, although this was something special even for him. The knife wounds Taja had inflicted were throbbing; at each jolt they took he hoped the stitches would hold.

Lola and Peter wore headphones. Silkie had taken hers off to get a better grip on her head with both hands.

"Where are we now?" Peter asked Lola.

"Over Blue Hill Bay. See that light down to our left?"

"Uh-huh," he said, his teeth clicking together.

"That's Bass Harbor head. Uh-oh. That's a Coast Guard cutter down there, steaming southwest. Somebody's got trouble. Take a dip in those waters tonight, you've got about twelve minutes. Okay, southwest is where we're heading now; right two-four-zero and closer to the deck. It's gonna get rougher, kids."

Peter checked the action of the old Colt Pocket Nine he'd borrowed from his Uncle Charlie in Brookline before heading up to Maine. Then he looked at islands appearing below. A lot of islands, some just specks on the IR.

"How are you going to find—"

"I know Kincairn by its light. Problem is, I don't think anyone's tried to land a helicopter there. Not a level spot on the island. Wind shear around a rock pile like Kincairn, conditions are just about perfect for an SOL funeral."

"SOL?" Silkie said. She'd put her headphones back on.

"Shit outa luck," Lola said, and laughed uproariously.

From a window of his study John Ransome observed through binoculars the lights in the studio flashing. A familiar sequence. Morse code distress signal. Mary Catherine's ingenuity made him smile. Of course he wouldn't have expected less of her. She was the last and the best of the Ransome women.

When he looked at the base of the Kincairn light, then down the road to the town, he saw one of the two Land Rovers he kept on the island coming up from the cove. When it stopped near the lighthouse, he wasn't surprised to see Taja get out.

Mary Catherine's face appeared behind salt-bleared glass, then vanished quickly, as if she'd seen Taja.

When the Woman in Black started toward the lighthouse, she walked slowly and stiffly, head lowered against the blasts of wind. She held her right side as if she'd been thrown around and injured while bringing the boat in through rough seas. Watching her, Ransome felt neither pity not regret. She was just a blight on his soul, as he had tried to explain to Mary Catherine. The time had come to remove it.

He put the binoculars down on his desk and unlocked a drawer. He kept an S&W police model .38 there. Hadn't fired the revolver in years but the bore was clean when he checked it.

Afterward a couple of phone calls and everything would be taken care of for him. As it always was. No messy publicity.

He felt deep empathy for Mary Catherine. It was unfortunate she had to be a part of the cleansing. But he would take care of her afterward, as he had all of the Ransome women. He had never used his genius as an excuse for poor behavior. When her own god failed her—as He would tonight—John Ransome would provide.

He was putting on his coat when he heard, above the wind, a helicopter fly low over the house.

"Peter, it's Taja!" Silkie yelled.

He saw the Woman in Black, looking up at the helicopter a hundred yards away. She had opened the door at the base of the lighthouse.

The studio lights were blinking again. Then Echo rushed to the windows, frantically signaling the helicopter.

"Who is that?" Silkie said.

"It's Echo," Peter said happily. Then, as Taja entered the lighthouse his momentary elation vanished. "Put us down!" he said to Lola.

"Not here! Maybe in the cove, on the dock!"

"How far's that?"

"Three miles south, I think."

"No! Can you drop me off here? Next to the lighthouse?"

"What are you doing?" Silkie asked anxiously.

"I can't maintain a hover more than three-four seconds," Lola advised him. "And not closer than ten feet off the ground!"

"Close enough!" Peter said. "Silkie! Go back with Lola. There's an APB out on Taja. Call the state cops, tell them she's on Kincairn!"

He opened the door on his side, looked at the rocks below in the undercarriage flood-light. The danger of it chilled him more than the wind in his face. If he landed wrong, a ten-foot jump onto frozen stony ground was going to feel like fifty.

In John Ransome's studio, Echo saw Taja get off the small elevator outside. They looked at each other for a few moments until Echo turned to the windows, seeing the helicopter fly away.

When she turned again Taja had unlocked the glass door and walked inside.

With the door open Echo's only thought was to get the hell out of there. But she couldn't get past Taja, who was quick and strong. An image of the PR boy in the subway repeated in Echo's mind as she was caught by one arm and pushed back. All the way to the easel that still held Ransome's beginning nude study of her. The portrait seemed to distract Taja as Echo struggled in her grip, swearing, swinging a wild left hand at the Woman in Black.

Taja's free hand came away from her side. The glove was sticky with blood. She groped behind her on the worktable. Her fingers closed on the handle of the knife that Ransome honed daily before trimming his brushes.

And Echo screamed.

Peter was halfway up the circular iron stairs, hobbling on a sprained ankle, when he heard the scream. Knew what it meant. But he was too slow and far from Echo to do her any good.

Taja struck once at Echo, slashing her across the heel of the hand Echo flung up to protect her face.

Then, instead of a lethal follow-up, Taja took the time to drive the knife into the canvas on the easel, ripping it in a gesture of fury.

Taja's body was momentarily at an angle to Echo, and vulnerable. Echo braced herself against the worktable and drove a knee high to the rib cage where Silkie had shot her in the Cambridge apartment.

Taja went down with a hoarse scream, dropped the knife. She was groping for it when Peter barreled into the studio and lunged at her.

"No, goddamn it, no!"

He grabbed her knife hand as she tried to come up off the floor at him. His free hand went to Taja's face, street-fighter style. He missed her eyes, tried to get a grip as she jerked her head aside.

Part of her flesh seemed to come loose in his hand. But it was only latex.

The face beneath her second skin was pocked with random, circular scars, as if from a dozen cigarette burns.

They were both hurt but Peter couldn't hold her. He knew the knife was coming. Then Echo got an armlock on Taja's neck and pulled her back; Peter stepped in with a short hook to Taja's jaw that dropped her instantly. He wrenched the knife away and pulled her back onto her feet. She wasn't unconscious but her eyes were crossing, no fight left in her.

"Let her go, Peter," John Ransome said behind them. "It's finished."

Peter shot a look behind him. "Not yet!" He looked again into Taja's eyes. "Tell me one thing! Was it Ransome? Did he send you after those women? Tell me!"

"Peter, she can't talk!" Echo said.

Taja still wasn't focusing. There was a

trickle of blood at one corner of her mouth.

"Find a way to talk to me! I want to know!"

"Peter," John Ransome said, "please let her go." His tone weary. "It's up to me to deal with Taja. She's my—"

"Was it Ransome!" Peter screamed in Taja's face, as she blinked, stared at him.

She nodded. Her eyes closed. A second later Ransome shot her. Blood and bits of bone from the hole in her forehead splattered Peter's face. She hung in his grip as Echo screamed. Still holding Taja up, Peter turned to Ransome, speechless with rage.

Ransome lowered his .38, taking a deep breath. "My responsibility. Sorry. Now will you put her down?"

Peter let Taja fall and went for his own gun, brought it up in both hands inches from Ransome's face.

"Drop your piece! So help me God I'll cap you right here!"

"Peter, no—!"

Ransome took another breath, his gun hand moving slowly toward the worktable, his finger off the trigger. "It's all right." He sounded eerily calm. I'm putting the gun down. Just don't let your emotions get the best of you. No accidents, Peter." The .38 was on the table. He lifted his hand slowly away from it, looked at Taja's body between them. Peter moved him at gunpoint back from the table.

"You're under arrest for murder! You have the right to remain silent. You have the right to be represented by an attorney. Anything you say can and will be used against you in a court of law. Do you understand what I've just said to you?"

Ransome nodded. "Peter, it was self-defense."

"Shut up, damn you! You don't get away with that!"

"You're out of your jurisdiction here. One more thing. I *own* this island."

"On your knees, hands behind your head."

"I think we need to talk when you're in a more rational—"

Peter took his finger off the trigger of the 9mm Colt and bounced it off the top of Ransome's head. Ransome staggered and dropped to one knee. He slowly raised his hands.

Peter glanced at Echo, who had pulled the sleeve of her sweater down over the hand that Taja had slashed. She'd made a fist to try to stop the bleeding. She shook from fear.

"Oh Peter, oh God! What are you going to do?"

"You own the island?" Peter said to Ransome. "Who cares? This is where we get off."

FIFTEEN

The boat Taja had used getting back and forth was a twenty-eight-foot Rockport-built island cruiser. Peter had John Ransome in the wheelhouse attached to a safety line with his hands lashed together in front of him. Echo was trying to hold the muzzle of the Colt 9mm on him while Peter battled wind gusts up to fifty knots and heavy seas once they left the shelter of Kincairn cove. In addition to the safety lines they all wore life vests. They were bucked all over the place. Peter found he could get only about eighteen knots from the Volvo diesel, and that it was nearly impossible to keep the wind on his stern unless he wanted to sail to Portugal. The wind chill was near zero. They were shipping a lot of water with a temperature of only a few degrees above freezing. The pounding went on without letup. Under reasonably good conditions it was thirty minutes to the mainland. Peter wasn't at all sure he had half an hour before hypothermia rendered him helpless.

John Ransome knew it. Watching Peter try to steer with one good hand, seeing Echo shaking with vomit on the front of her life vest, he said, "We won't make it. Breathe through your nose, Mary Catherine, or you'll freeze your lungs. You know I don't want you to die like this! Talk sense to Peter! Best of times it's like threading a needle through all the little islands. In a blow you can lose your boat on the rocks."

"Peter's s-sailed b-boats all his life!"

Ransome shook his head. "Not under these conditions."

A vicious gust heeled them to port; the bow was buried in a cornering wave. Water cascaded off the back of the overhead as the cruiser righted itself sluggishly.

"Peter!"

"We're okay!" he yelled, leaning on the helm.

Ransome smiled in sympathy with Echo's terror.

"We're not okay." He turned to Peter. "There is a way out of this dilemma, Peter! If you'd only give me a chance to make things right for all of us! But you must turn back *now*!"

"I told you, I don't have dilemmas! Echo, keep that gun on him!"

Ransome said, his eyes on the shivering girl, "I don't think Peter knows you as well as I've come to know you, Mary Catherine! You couldn't shoot me. No matter what you think I've done."

Echo, her eyes red from salt, raised the muzzle of the Colt unsteadily as she tried to keep from slipping off the bench opposite Ransome.

"Which one—are you tonight?" she said bitterly. "The g-god who creates, or the god who destroys?"

They were taking on water faster than the pump could empty the boat. The cruiser wallowed, nearly directionless.

"Remember the rogue wave, Mary Catherine? You saved me then. Am I worth saving now?"

"Don't listen to him!" Peter rubbed his eyes, trying to focus through the spume on the wheelhouse window. What he saw momentarily and some distance away were the running lights of a large yacht or even a cutter. Because of the cold he had only limited use of his left hand. His wrist had begun bleeding again during his fight with Taja at the lighthouse. With numbed fingers he was able to open a locker in front of him. "Echo, this guy has fucked up every life he ever touched!"

"There's no truth in that! It was Taja, no matter what she wanted you to believe. Her revenge on me. And I was the only one who ever cared about her! Mary Catherine, last night I tried to stop her from going after Silkie MacKenzie! You know what happened. But the story of Taja and myself is not easy to explain. You understand, though, don't you?"

"You should have seen what I've seen the last forty-eight hours, Echo! The faces of Ransome's women. Slashed, burned, broken! Two that I know of are dead! Nan

McLaren OD'd, Ransome—you hear about that?"

"Yes. Poor Nan—but I—"

"Last night Valerie Angelus went off the roof of her building! You set her up for that, you son of a bitch!"

Ransome lifted his head.

"But you could've stopped her. A year, two years ago, it wouldn't have been too late for Valerie! You didn't want her. Don't talk about caring, it makes me sick!"

Ransome lunged off his bench toward Echo and easily took the automatic from her half-frozen hands. He turned toward Peter with it but lost his footing. Peter abandoned the helm, kicked the Colt into the stern of the boat, then pointed a Kilgore flare pistol, loaded with a twenty-thousand-candlepower parachute flare, at Ransome's head.

"I think the Coast Guard's out there to starboard," Peter said. "If you make a big enough bonfire they'll see it."

"The flare will only destroy my face," Ransome said calmly. "I suppose you would consider that to be justice." On his knees, Ransome held up his bound hands suppliantly. "We could have settled this among ourselves. Now it's too late." He looked at Echo. "*Is* it too late, Mary Catherine?"

She was sitting in a foot of water on the deck, exhausted, just trying to hold on as the boat rolled violently. She looked at him, and looked away. "Oh God, John."

Ransome struggled to his feet. "Take the helm, Peter, or she'll roll over! And the two of you may still have a life together."

"Just shut up, Ransome!"

He smiled. "You're both very young. Some day I hope you will learn that the greater part of wisdom is . . . forgiveness."

He unclipped his safety line from the vest as the bow of the cruiser rose, letting the motion carry him backwards to the transom railing. Where he threw himself overboard, vanishing into the pitch-dark water.

Echo cried out, a wail of despair, then sobbed. Peter felt nothing other than a cold indifference to the fate the artist had chosen. He raised the flare pistol and fired it, then returned to the helm as the flare shed its light upon the water, bringing nearby islands into jagged relief. A few moments later they heard a siren through the low scream of wind; a searchlight probed the darkness and found them. Peter closed his eyes in the glare and leaned against the helm with Echo laid against his back, arms around him.

Below decks of the Coast Guard cutter as it returned to the station on Mount Desert Island with the cruiser in tow, a change in pitch in the cutter's engine and a shudder that ran through the vessel caused Echo to wake up in a cocoon of blankets. She jerked violently.

"Easy," Peter said. He was sitting beside her on the sick bay rack, holding her hand.

"Where are we?"

"Coming in, I guess. You okay?"

She licked her chapped lips. "I think so. Peter, are we in trouble?"

"No. I mean, there's gonna be a hell of an inquiry. We'll take what comes and say what is. Want coffee?"

"No. Just want to sleep."

"Echo, I have to know—"

"Can't talk now," she protested wanly.

"Maybe we should. Get it out of the way, you know? Just say what is. Either way, I promise I can deal with it."

She blinked, looked at him with ghostly eyes, raised her other hand to gently touch his face.

"I posed for him—well, you saw the work Taja took a knife to."

"Yeah."

She took a deep breath. Peter was like stone.

"I didn't sleep with him, Peter."

After a few moments he shrugged. "Okay."

"But—no—I want to tell you all of it. Peter, I was getting ready to. Another couple of days, a week—it would've happened."

"Oh, Jesus."

"I just needed to be with him. But I didn't love him. It's something I—I don't think I'll ever understand about myself. I'm sorry."

Peter shook his head, perplexed, dismayed. She waited tensely for the anger. Instead he put his arms around her.

"You don't have to be sorry. I know what he was. And I know what I saw—in the eyes of those other women. I don't see it in your eyes." He kissed her. "He's gone. And that's all I care about."

A second kiss, and her glum face lost its anxiety, she began to lighten up.

"I do love you. Infinity."

"Infinity," he repeated solemnly. "Echo?"

"Yes?"

"I looked at a sublet before I left the city a few days ago. Fully furnished loft in Williamsburg. Probably still available. Fifteen hundred a month. We can move in by Christmas."

"Hey. Fifteen? We can swing that." She smiled slightly, teasing. "Live in sin for a little while, that what you mean?"

"Just live," he said.

On a Sunday in mid-April, four weeks before their wedding, Peter and Echo, enjoying each other's company and one of life's minor enchantments, which was to laze with no purpose, heard the elevator in their building start up.

"Company?" Peter said. He was watching the Knicks on TV.

"Mom and Julia aren't coming until four," Echo said. She was doing tai chi exercises on a floor mat, barefoot, wearing only gym shorts. The weather in Brooklyn was unseasonably warm.

"Then it's nobody," Peter said. "But maybe you should pull on a top anyhow."

He walked across the painted floor of the loft they shared and watched the elevator rising toward them. In the dimness of the shaft he couldn't make out anyone in the cage.

When it stopped he pulled up the gate and looked inside. A wrapped package leaned against one side of the elevator. About three feet by five. Brown paper, tape, twine.

"Hey, Echo?"

She wriggled into a halter top and came over to look. Her lips parted in astonishment.

"It's a painting. Omigod!"

"What?"

"Get it! Open it!"

Peter lugged the wrapped painting, which seemed to be framed, to the table in their kitchen. Echo followed with scissors and cut the twine.

"But it can't be! There's no way—! No, be careful, let me do this!"

She removed the thick paper and laid the painting flat on the table.

"Oh no," Peter groaned. "I don't believe this. He's back."

The painting was John Ransome's self-portrait that had been hanging in the artist's library on Kincairn when Echo had last seen it.

Echo turned it over. On the back Ransome had inscribed, "Given to Mary Catherine Halloran as a remembrance of our friendship." It was signed and dated two days before Ransome's disappearance.

She turned suddenly, shoving Peter aside, and ran to the loft windows that overlooked a cobbled mews and afforded a partial view of the Brooklyn Bridge, with lower Manhattan beyond.

"Peterrrr!"

He caught up to her, looked over her shoulder and down at the mews. There were kids playing, a couple of women with strollers. And a man in a black topcoat getting into a cab on the corner where the fruit and vegetable stand was doing brisk business. The man had shoulder-length gray hair and wore dark glasses. That was all they could see of him.

Peter looked at Echo as the cab drove away. Touched her shoulder until she focused on him, on the here and now.

"He drowned, Echo."

She turned with a broad gesture in the direction of the portrait. "But—"

"Maybe his body never turned up, but the water—we nearly froze ourselves on the boat. His hands were tied. Telling you, no way he survived."

"John told me he swam the Hellespont once. The Dardanelles strait. That's at least a couple miles across. And hypothermia—everybody's tolerance of cold is different. Sailors have survived for hours in seas that probably would kill you or me in fifteen minutes." She gestured again, excited. "Peter—who else?"

"Maybe it was somebody works for Cy Mellichamp. That slick son of a bitch. Just having his little joke. Listen, I don't want the damn picture in our house. I don't want to be reminded, Echo. How you got short-changed on your contract. None of it." He waited. "Do you?"

"Well—" She looked around their loft. Shrugged. "I guess it wouldn't be, uh, appropriate. But obviously—it was meant as a wedding gift." She smiled strangely. "All I did was say how much I admired his self-portrait. John told me all about it. There's quite a story goes with it, which would make the painting especially valuable to a collector. It's unique in the Ransome canon."

"Yeah? How valuable?"

"Hard to say. I know a Ransome was knocked down recently at Christie's for just under five million dollars."

Peter didn't say anything.

"The fact that his body hasn't been recovered complicated matters for his estate. But," Echo said judiciously, "as Stefan put it, 'it certainly has done no harm to the value of his art.'"

"You want a beer?"

"I would love a beer."

Echo remained by the windows looking out while Peter went to the refrigerator. While he was popping tops he said, "So—figure we just put the portrait away in a closet a couple years, then it could be worth a shitload?"

"Oh baby," Echo replied.

"Then, also in a couple years," Peter said, coming back to her and carefully fitting a can of Heineken into her hand, "when Ransome's estate gets settled, that cottage in Bedford, which looks like a pretty nice investment, will go on the market?"

"Might." Echo took a long drink of the beer and began laughing softly, ironically, to herself.

"All this could depend on, you know, he doesn't turn up." Peter looked out the window. "Again."

The last Ransome woman was silent. Wondering, lost in a private rapture.

Peter said, "You want to order in Chinese for Rosemay and Julia tonight? I've still got a few bucks left on my MasterCard."

"Yeah," Echo said, and leaned her head on his shoulder. "Chinese. Sounds good."